I0626615

The Murder of the U.S.A.

By

Will F. Jenkins

Here is an entirely new kind of murder mystery — with a whole nation as the victim. Imagine a sudden mysterious atomic attack on the United States. Imagine one third of the nation destroyed in forty minutes. Imagine being unable to determine the location of the enemy.

In a series of thrilling climaxes, Sam Burton and his cohorts in Burrow 89, operating under imminent danger of being blown to bits, manage to discover the murderer, and end the holocaust. Will F. Jenkins has here turned his pen to the problem of atomic war, has presented the probable defenses, and at the same time has created one of the most dramatic and exciting detective yarns ever written.

THE
Murder
OF THE
U.S.A.

By
WILL F. JENKINS

WILDSIDE PRESS

Copyright © 1946 by Will F. Jenkins.

To JOHN W. CAMPBELL, JR.

*Whose belief in this story, from the beginning,
is the reason for the existence of this book.*

1

*M*ORE THAN A THIRD OF THE PEOPLE OF the United States never knew anything about the war—not even that it had happened. Their share in it was too short.

The first bombs landed at 11:10 A.M. Washington time, and for forty minutes they continued to drop by ones and twos and half-dozens out of empty space beyond the atmosphere. While they fell, the Army radars all over the country showed them as small moving specks darting into detection-range upon invariable courses, all due south. Bombs moved due south to drop on San Francisco, and due south to hit Chicago, and due south to New

York and Dubuque and Phoenix and New Orleans. All the courses fanned out with mathematical exactitude from the geographic North Pole—which was actually a way-point, not their launching-site— and altogether there were between two and three hundred of them. At 11:50 Washington time (but by then there wasn't any Washington) they stopped, and all the radar screens again showed unchanging patterns. The moving specks had vanished. But so had the cities of the United States.

There were said to be a few tall buildings inexplicably still standing in Chicago, but it could not be verified. There seemed to be some survivors in San Francisco, too, due probably to a blast-shadow cast by Nob Hill. But the rest of the cities of America were simply erased. There was just one of over 100,000 population still intact, and six above 50,000 that had not been bombed. Four below 25,000 had been blasted, because they had well-known war industries, and some smaller communities as well. These little targets were also understandable. They were villages supplying labor to certain critical mines, and isolated factories turning out vaccines and biologicals, and one or two research laboratories with highly-trained staffs. The

4

only apparent oddity in the choice of targets was the blasting of lakes. Nearly every sizeable mountain lake in the United States received an atomic bomb from outer space, and the radioactive matter which poured into American river-systems was later a major problem in itself.

Essentially, however, the bombs concentrated on the larger cities. That was why more than one-third of America's population never knew anything about the war at all. One instant they were alive; the next, they weren't. Some few individuals may have seen instantaneous flares of light a thousand times brighter than the sun. There may even have been persons who momentarily felt an intolerable radiant heat, as from the opened door of a blast-furnace. But even they did not really know what was happening. They had no reason to expect bombing. There was no unusual diplomatic strain between the United States and any other country. The whole thing was a complete and effective surprise, and the bombs on that account were a highly merciful weapon. The people who were killed by them were not even frightened beforehand.

But almost two-thirds of the population re-mained alive — and the Burrows remained, too.

They had been designed to survive even such a catastrophe as this, and to avenge it. Of all of them, only eight were smashed in the first bombing, and they were destroyed by direct hits. The rest . . .

Waited. There was nothing else to do.

2

$\mathcal{F}$OURTEEN HOURS AFTER THE BOMBS
fell, Lieutenant Sam Burton watched a television screen grimly. He was acting adjutant of
Burrow 89, officially Rocket Missile Launching Base
Number Eighty-Nine of the Atomic Counter-Attack Force, U. S. The television screen showed the
surface above the Burrow. The control-room from
which he watched was under four hundred feet of
solid rock; that rock was under the moving icy mass
of Ranier Glacier on Mount Harrow in the Rockies;
and the television screen showed the tumbled,
striated mass of the ice-river which concealed Burrow 89 from thermal detectors in the stratosphere.

The screen gave glimpses of the tall and naked mountains between which Ranier Glacier flowed. It gave small peeps at the cold blue sky from which atomic bombs had plunged upon America. But the thing on which Sam Burton's eyes were fixed was a group of three moving specks on the glacier's surface. They were human beings. They were apparently trying to cross the glacier. And today — with the nation fallen into chaos — was no time for innocent sports like mountain-climbing. The three figures were disturbing. They might be spies. Since the Brienne Agreement of all the United Nations, by which each one pledged itself to use atomic bombs ruthlessly on any disturber of the world's peace, espionage had become a major industry. Defense in a normal sense against atomic bombs was an impossibility. So the Burrows* were built to make even successful attack futile. They could not stop

* "Burrow." The popular and almost universal name given to the underground rocket-launching stations of the Atomic Service. They were christened in a Congressional speech by Senator Buffington (Ind. Idaho) who in combatting the appropriations proposed for them referred scornfully to the "burrows for our supposedly gallant troops to hide in like rats." Senator Buffington was in Boise, Idaho, when the city was destroyed, attending a conference called by Senator Burton K. Wheeler to plan for the withdrawal of the United States from the Brienne Agreement.

an atomic bomb attack, but they could repay it with interest, and the interest might amount to annihilation. Unless, of course, the Burrows of the attacked nation had been marked down for destruction and were destroyed through data secured by spies.

That was the point at the present moment. Eight Burrows had been destroyed by direct hits in the first bombing. In the following fourteen hours nine others had been obliterated. Now there were three ant-sized figures struggling across Ranier Glacier. If they were spies, their presence meant that Burrow 89 would shortly follow the other smashed seventeen into nothingness. If they detected the heat produced by the deuterium pile which provided all the power for the Burrow's needs* a bomb would shortly come plunging out of space. It would travel at four miles a second on arrival. The detection-devices could be certain of its target thirty seconds before its landing, but no earlier. And Burrow 89 would disappear in a splash of flame which would reach the stratosphere.

The logical thing, then, was to kill these three figures. Now. Without parley or delay. The func-

---

* Data on the deuterium pile and its power output may be found in "Atomic Energy for Military Purposes" (The Smyth Report), p. 147, and elsewhere.

tioning of the Burrow was more important than human lives, even those of innocent citizens. But it also followed that if they were spies, to kill them might disclose to other spies that they had been killed, and hence also reveal the existence of the Burrow.

Lieutenant Sam Burton watched them savagely. All over the continent, the Burrows still waited. Since the destruction of America as a nation, not one rocket had left a launching tube in reply. Not so much as a cap-pistol had been fired in retaliation for the murder of seventy million Americans. For the enemy, the murderer nation, was still unknown. The United States had not been defeated in war. It had been assassinated.

A loud-speaker muttered over at one side of the control-room instrument-board. Even as he watched the vision-screen, Sam's left hand slowly moved the dial of a speech-set (without television) tuned to the wave-bands assigned to radio amateurs. Save for the communication system by which the Burrows kept in touch with each other, and certain surviving Army mobile units, the amateur radio operators of the United States constituted the only means by which the separated fragments of a nation could hear news, because news normally originated in cities and was disseminated from them.

When Washington vanished in a burst of flame, the means by which the news of the event should have reached — say — Chicago, vanished with Washington. Chicago turned into something resembling a section of the sun's photosphere with no inkling of any untoward event elsewhere, and Los Angeles disappeared between two seconds without even a radioed suspicion that the Gulf of Mexico was roaring in to fill a great chasm where New Orleans had stood, or that the site of Manhattan Island had become a bubbling, boiling bay.

All the normal means of transmitting news vanished with the cities, and more than population and teletype service vanished with them. With its cities gone, America fell apart into a myriad isolated, crumbling small municipalities. No unit of government larger than a small municipality remained. No railroad ran. No power line functioned. No broadcasting station remained on the air. In forty minutes of bombing it became impossible to send a letter, a telegram, or a loaf of bread from one place to another in America. But the radio amateurs remained — those who did not live in cities. Voices of

all sorts came out of the speaker unit while Lieutenant Sam Burton watched the figures on the
glacier.

Somebody repeated desperately: *"Anybody on the
West Coast please answer! My girl's visiting in Pasadena. Has it been hit?"* Another voice said stolidly,
*"For general information, the cities in the New
England area known to have been bombed are
Aroostook, Bangor, Boston —"* The dial moved on.
An earnest voice announced: *"The amateur relay
operators urgently request clearance of the addi-
tional bands just mentioned for messages between
surviving towns. Please change your frequencies,
you fellows on those bands!"* The dial moved on
again. A new voice said, *"Reporting to whatever
authorities there may be, an atomic flare was seen
over the Bookshelf Mountains half an hour ago.
Sound-wave and concussion followed, indicating an
atomic explosion twenty-five miles southeast of —"*
Then the first voice cut in hysterically on a new
wave-length. *"Anybody on the West Coast please
answer! My girl's visiting in Pasadena. Has it been
hit?"*

Sam Burton continued to watch the figures on
the screen. They struggled to get across the piled-up,

pinnacled mass of ice where Ranier Glacier curved and the ice tried vainly to ripple, and instead made a surface almost impossible to cross. The three figures were roped together. The one in the middle was slimmer than the others. It moved agilely enough, but even at a distance which made it a bare speck, somehow it seemed unlike its companions. It might be a girl.

The door opened. Major Fred Thale came in. He was Sam Burton's friend, and by the same accident that had made Sam the acting adjutant, he was commanding officer of the Burrow. His face was queerly blank — and gray. But he said with a detached precision, "Anything yet, Sam?"

Sam pointed to the screen. The figures struggled hopelessly across fissured, tumbled masses of ice.

"They're still there. We're listening to them with every radiation-set in the place. They're not sending anything on any wave-band we know of. They could be a pleasure party who'd heard about what's happened on a pocket receiver, trying to take a short-cut back to civilization. But they could be spies, too. We could heave a charge of high-explosive at them and wipe them out. But that might provide a signal that somebody didn't want them around here, and that there must be a Burrow nearby. We can leave them alone, possibly to find out we're down here and signal that. We could bring them in here, and if they're spies possibly find out whom they're spying for. But they may have some trick communicator we don't know about, and their stopping signalling might bring a bomb."

"They might be regular people too, Sam," said Thale wearily. "We don't want to kill our own sort. We'll wait a while. What else?"

"I've been listening to the radio hams," Sam replied. "There's been no invasion yet. An atom bomb went off in the Bookshelf Mountains. Probably a Burrow smashed. Centralia was bombed an hour ago. Thurston—Secretary of Agriculture—was the only cabinet member not in Washington, so he automatically became President. He was on his way to his farm in Ohio when the bombs fell. One blotted out his farm, by the way. But like a damned fool he located an Army mobile transmitter and had it announce his succession to the Presidency and that Centralia would be our temporary capital. A bomb landed an hour and twenty-five minutes later. Did you get any sleep?"

Thale shook his head. His expression was dazed.

Even when it was obvious that he was forcing careful attention, his features tended to relax into an absent, puzzled expression. It held no grief, only a tragic bewilderment.

"I couldn't sleep," he said heavily. "I could have taken something to make me, of course, but it would slow up my thinking. I still can't believe it, Sam. Stella went off to visit her mother, and she and the kid were grinning and waving when the tube-car pulled out. And they—reached St. Louis before the bomb fell there."

"Tough," said Sam perfunctorily. With over a third of America dead and the rest in chaos, this was no time for emotionalism.

Thale shook his head, as though to clear it. "That kid," he said. "She was crazy about Little Black Sambo. You know Sambo: 'Once upon a time there was a little black boy, and his name was Little Black Sambo—' "

Sam stood up. When he spoke, his voice was cold and impersonal.

"You're the commanding officer of this Burrow, Fred. There's a war on, and Burrows are being bombed. By the rules of the Atomic Service nobody can give you any orders from now until peacetime comes. You can only be advised. I advise you to get going on our course of action. It's the only way to stand your own loss."

His eyes jerked to the vision-screen. One of the three figures had vanished.

"Look at that!"

The other two figures were motionless. After an instant one of them moved slowly and cautiously. It stopped. The second moved. Three minutes later the missing figure reappeared. It stumbled and fell. The other two closed with it. They worked upon it. After a little, the three figures moved forward again. They were in a compact group, now. Two of them supported the third. They were in the midst of a monstrous untrodden wilderness, on the surface of a glacier they were attempting to cross. They had nearly completed the most difficult part of their journey, but soon they would enter upon the area most certainly trapped with crevasses covered over with snow.

"Whether they're spies or not," said Sam, "they're sunk. Using ropes, they might have made it. All of them bunched together like that, they won't."

A pneumatic tube hissed and then popped loudly, four feet down the control-board. Thale moved slowly over to pick up the message-carrier. He pulled out the scribbled sheet from Communications—the room where men and Wacs ran recording machines covering every imaginable wave-band, and then examined every word and signal on the air. He read it. Then he turned to Sam.

"A radio ham in Sun Valley reports that there are a bunch of consular and diplomatic officials there—minor attachés, mainly, on vacation. They asked him to put it on the relay circuit so they'll be picked up. If they aren't bombed within a couple of hours we'll see what we can do. We could use the heli. We could use them too."

Sam continued to watch the stumbling, laboring figures on the vision-screen.

"I've got a hunch, Fred," he said suddenly.

Thale raised his eyes.

"A hunch on the nature of war," said Sam. "If you and I were mountain-climbing, and the third member of our party got lamed, we'd stay with him. Even if it practically meant that we wouldn't get back. Decency is more important than survival, in a case like that. Right?"

Thale nodded.

"So?"

"If you and I were spies, trying to find a Burrow for our side to bomb, and our companion got lamed, we'd leave him. We'd have to. Because our job as spies would be more important than decency in a case like that. But these people are sticking together. So they probably aren't spies."

Thale nodded again.

"It's practically dark on the surface," he said. "When it's full-dark you can use the heli and go get them."

Sam stood up.

"I'm off," he announced. "It'll take a little while to get set for the job."

He left the control-room and threaded his way through the underground labyrinth which was the Burrow. It contained all the elements of a city: living-quarters, eating-places, recreation-centers— even hydroponic gardens and a power-plant which was a deuterium pile ceaselessly making more atomic explosive for the bombs in the storage-rooms far below even this level. Naturally, the Burrow had equipment for flying, though in peacetime no helicopter had ever flown from the concealed exit-port high above the floor of the glacier.

Now that war had come, though, risks were inevitable. So Sam Burton summoned the ready-trained helicopter crew and went to the hitherto unused hangar. It took a little time to check the machine, to issue equipment and to give specific orders. Then the machine and crew began the long, long rise on the lift to the point from which the helicopter could fly.

The lift stopped. Sam examined the outer world from television scanners within the seemingly solid rock. Night had fallen and the last least trace of afterglow was gone. He threw over a control. There was a small, almost inaudible creaking, and the stone roof rose straight up. The helicopter rose with it. It lay, then, in the open air beneath a monster boulder upheld on four steel pillars. Its motor started soundlessly. It ran forward, out from beneath the concealing stone. Before it lay the twisting, luminous glacier.

The helicopter took off in absolute quiet. Clinging to the mountain flank, it swept down and away. Presently it swung about and started up the length of the glacier again. Somewhere in fifty square miles of ice there were three human beings. They might be spies, or they might not. If they were not spies, their lives would be saved. If they were spies, it was possible that something might be learned from them that would make it possible to avenge, in kind and in degree, the murder of more than one-third of America.

3

STARS SHONE BRIGHT AND UNWINKING
between the surrounding mountain peaks. It was
high, here over the glacier, and the air was thin and
very cold. There were patches of faintly glowing
white rearing upward toward the sky—snow-fields on
the mountain flanks. The helicopter's cabin was
comfortable enough, but all about it there was only
frigidity and hills and faint starlight filtering gently
down upon a frozen world. Sam found himself thinking with a bitter irony of a Christmas carol. *"Silent
night, holy night . . ."* All about was calm and bright.
But under the glacier the Burrow waited savagely.
The tranquillity of the mountains was mockery.

The pilot of the helicopter watched a little square screen, in which the terrain about showed as the infra-red detector* saw it—by heat rays which it turned to light upon its screen. It was a picture of the landscape, not in terms of light and shade or color, but of temperature.

A man behind Sam said softly to another, "You think they're crazy enough to invade?"

"I dunno," said the other man grimly," but I'm prayin' for it. That's all I'm askin' of Gawd just now. Just let 'em start invadin'! Then we'll know who they are an' we'll start shootin'!"

The helicopter clung to the mountain flank and went far, far down the glacier's length before it swung out into the center and swept back toward the three it was to snatch from the ice. It flew low.

---

* An infra-red detector, of a sort, is used to penetrate fog. For military use, an infra-red detector is a device which makes a picture of an area by the use of a hypersensitive bolometer which records the infra-red radiation of an object simply as energy. They have an advantage over Johnson detectors (see later) in their greater accuracy in determining the temperature of a distant object, and share with them the very great advantage of not emitting any signal of their own, as radar has to do, in order to perceive things at a distance. However, radar does read off distance and hence speed. When concealment is unnecessary or impossible, it has advantages too.

If by any chance any enemy device were scanning this area, a dot fifty feet above such a tumbled surface would be far less conspicuous than at a normal flying height.

The infra-red screen pictured an unearthly landscape, in which snow was black and bare rock faintly luminous, because of their relative temperatures. Presently a minute bright speck appeared. That was the vastly warmer (by comparison) bodies of the three people on the glacier. The flying-machine changed course. It swept on, trailing a swirling snow-devil behind it as its down-draft beat upon the snow. The bright speck grew in size upon the screen. Details appeared, with all light and shade reversed as in a photographic negative.

The three figures were huddled together for warmth. They had ceased to try to move forward. They lay in the lee of an ice-hummock, hoping to stay alive until morning.

Sam gave sharp orders. The heli landed a quarter-mile away, down-wind. Four men, with Sam, tumbled out, wearing snow-shoes. The helicopter rose soundlessly, while the snow from its down-draft rose blindingly. The five moved forward, and it hovered above and behind. The voice of the pilot sounded tinnily in headphones under the parka-helmet of each man.

Sam waved his men to right and left. They wore white garments, almost invisible against the snow, but plainly apparent to the pilot on the infra-red screen. They moved up-wind, with the voice in the headphones guiding them. They encircled the three figures without once sighting them. They closed in, on instructions from above.

The actual moment of contact was sudden and fierce and necessarily brutal. They plunged upon those they had come to rescue; they seized them savagely and held them helpless. In particular, they made sure that none of the three lost ones touched their own bodies with their hands.

The helicopter dropped in a blinding upsurge of rotor-driven snow. The three figures, struggling, were dragged into the ship, which rose again and went into insane antics, skittering here and there barely above the snow like an intoxicated dragon-fly. Its downward slip-stream erased all footprints and the signs of its landing, undermining packed snowshoe-prints and leaving nothing but such a crazy trail as an erratic eddy might have made. Then it went on, not for the Burrow or its hangar, but on a completely deceptive course.

In the cabin, the three rescued humans were swiftly and quite ruthlessly examined for metal objects, more particularly for anything that could send an electronic signal. Sam ignored the look of startled, panicky recognition in the eyes of the girl who was one of the three.

"You're safe enough if you aren't spies," he stated, staring coldly at her as though he had never seen her before. "We're Atomic Service. We took a chance and picked you up when our detector spotted you on the ice. If you're spies, you're going to talk. If you're not, you've nothing to worry about."

He turned away. The three captives sat dazed and still, under the grim scrutiny of three crewmen. They had been picked up no more than a mile and a half from the launching-point of the helicopter, but it was thirty minutes before the silent craft settled down beside its port. The prisoners could have no faintest idea of the direction or the distance they had traveled. The craft rolled in under the monstrous rock. The rock descended. The lift dropped aircraft and crew and passengers down into the bowels of the earth.

Fifteen minutes later Sam opened the control-room door and went in. Thale looked up.

"Got 'em," said Sam. He went on slowly, "Two men and a girl. I used to know the girl, Thale. I don't know—I hate to believe it—but it looks bad to me. I've set a couple of Wacs to watch her. One of the men has a torn ligament from a fall. News?"

Thale shook his head.

"Forty-seven isn't in communication," he replied. "That was probably the Bookshelf explosion. Whoever's hitting at us has something, and God knows what it is, but they're spotting Burrows and blasting them. If they get enough of us . . ."

Both of them had ignored the constant muttering of the loud-speaker on which radio ham broadcasts—the only broadcasts anywhere—came through. Now a voice snapped, "*Q R H! Q R H! Emergency! An atom-bomb flare just went up somewhere in the Sierras. We're counting seconds now for the sound-wave. The nearest city in the line of the flare is—*" The voice stopped. An indistinguishable roaring noise. "*There's the sound-wave! We weren't on the air when the flare was noted, but we've been counting seconds ever since. The bomb landed . . .*" The voice gave exact coordinates, carefully not naming its own location.

"Another Burrow," said Thale. "Somebody's got something, all right. They're sniping us to hell and gone. It looks like they had every Burrow mapped. But why didn't they blast us first of all?"

Sam Burton's voice was suddenly hard.

"The people I brought in are spies. This is no time for niceties. Let's find out what they know."

A pneumatic message-carrier popped out of its tube. Thale picked out the rolled scrap of paper.

"One-O-Two ceased communication in the middle of a message," he said in a dry voice. "Eight Burrows smashed in the first bombing. Isn't this twelve more since? Those bastards may win this war without our even knowing who they are."

There was a pause. Then he added, "I'll send a helicopter for those people at Sun Valley, Sam. It's not certain, of course, but if any of them refuses to come to a Burrow it might be informative—if we take note of his nationality. Only our enemies know the Burrows are being bombed."

He spoke into a transmitter. He stopped and looked up.

"You'll take the heli this time too, Sam?"

"I stay here!" said Sam sourly. "Send somebody who doesn't know about Burrows being smashed!

Anyhow, I want to talk to those people we picked up. I know the girl, damn her! Damn her and all the other slick customers we've ever trusted!"

He began to pace up and down the control-room. He was suddenly, horribly enraged. The finding of Betty Clarke on the glacier somehow crystalized it. Spies would be the deciding factor in this war, and she was a spy. He shook with fury and a maddening sense of futility. The Burrows had been built for exactly this basic situation. Since there could be no defense against atomic bombs, the only possible deterrent would be the certainty of terrible and adequate revenge. But the bombs had fallen seventeen hours since, and there was still no revenge. There was no indication of who had sent them, and spies were marking down Burrows for destruction, ending even the hope of vengeance.

And the girl was a spy. There could be no doubt about it. However he'd once felt about her—whatever dreams it was now bitterness to recall—she was a spy. The evidence was overwhelming. And an Atomic Service officer had an obligation that would not let him deceive himself. If she was a spy, and if she had contributed to the murder of the United States . . .

Sam Burton resumed his pacing.

Wars had started in ancient days as migrations. Later they developed into raids for slaves and loot—a primitive type of war later revived by Germany and Japan. In the Middle Ages and until the late Eighteenth Century, wars were a stately if horrible form of the duello. But this war was simply murder, by a criminal desperately resolved to avoid detection.

All the world knew it. All the world knew what the Burrows waited for. All earth was in a panic lest they loose their bombs upon a nation which was innocent of the assassination of America. No government anywhere remained seated in its own capital for as long as one hour after the news of the war was received. The British government was "somewhere in the neighborhood of Stratford-on-Avon" and at twenty-minute intervals repeated to America and the world that it was prepared to fulfill the Brienne Agreement to the letter. Its Burrows, not only on the home island but in every Dominion, would attack the murderer nation as soon as proof of guilt was forthcoming. The French government announced from "somewhere in

France" that it, too, was prepared to meet its commitments made at Brienne. Belgium, Holland—even the Scandinavian countries and Switzerland—had the rocket-tubes of their hidden fortresses ready. Spain was poorly prepared, and Bulgaria could add little to the storm of annihilation which—of sheer necessity—must follow American bombs upon the country proved guilty of war. But little Greece was murderously ready, and Poland and Czechoslovakia. And Russia firmly declared that the war waged upon America was war declared upon all humanity.

Yet, one of the protesting nations—and *all* were vociferously ready to destroy the breaker of the world's peace—was that peace-breaker itself. That one must be ready to rend and tear all the world beyond itself if or when it was unmasked. So cities, everywhere, went mad with terror.

At any moment all earth might flame into atomic war. The city-dwellers of every continent rose in crazy panic and tried to escape from their cities. Slum dwellers—more instantly capable of desperation—looted and killed on the way to open country. In London every avenue from the city was choked with human beings, so tightly wedged together that corpses of people killed by suffocation were held up and carried forward by the mass, which moved at the most agonizing of crawls.

In Paris, waves of panic swept over a completely hysterical public. The Place St. Dominique unhappily formed the focus of four avenues which fed fugitives into it, while a single narrow street led toward the suburbs. It was filled to bursting. To stumble was to fall, and to fall was to die. Where the pressure was greatest—at the entrance to the narrow street—there was a terrible mound over which those who passed down the street must climb. The mound reached from house-wall to house-wall and was ten feet high. It had been human beings. . . .

In Naples, men banded together and cut ways through crushed and immobilized humanity by the use of knives. Even in Switzerland the city folk went mad with fear. In Stockholm the city's bridges collapsed under the frenzied throngs fleeing to the open country. Protective railings—even those of stone—were forced out by the press of bodies. Literally thousands were crushed into the water. Most of them died.

The death toll in Athens came to thousands more. In Sofia, in Istanbul, in Moscow, in Odessa, in

Stalingrad and Helsingfors and Oslo and Copenhagen; in Lisbon and Barcelona and Palermo and Madrid. . . . There were corpses everywhere under the feet of crowds which screamed senselessly and fought more senselessly still, and swayed here and there in the blind stark panic of those who feel death peering down at them from the rooftops. The loss of life in Europe was appalling. It had already equalled the death toll of a sizeable war in the pre-atomic tradition. But of course it was still trivial compared with that in America.

Sam paused in his pacing.

"What do the detectors say about the bombs that are nosing out our Burrows?"

"Naturally, we're only using Johnson detectors* and infra-red scanners so far," Thale replied, "but

* Johnson detector; a highly sensitive microwave receiver, capable of detecting a part of the infra-red radiations of any warm body as ultra-short radio waves. The "Johnson effect" was observed by Dr. Johnson of the Bell Telephone Laboratories during the last year of the Second World War (the first atomic war) and received his name. The essence of Dr. Johnson's discovery was that every natural object is by reason of its temperature a radiator—a transmitter—of ultra-short but very real radio waves. The detector bearing his name makes use of this fact to locate and differentiate between distant objects.

the Army radars on the surface are still working and broadcasting their patterns for us to pick up. There are too many of them to bomb, though they can be located easily enough. They say the bombs are still coming due south. They fly to the North Pole, change course, and come due south for their targets."

"But dammit, they've got to fly to the North Pole! They've got to be detectable on the way there!"

"Beyond the atmosphere? Yes. But they have to be sorted out from radar indications of meteoric particles. There are always plenty of them! My guess would be that the sniper-bombs are coming from mid-ocean somewhere, or there might have been a cache of them flown to the middle of the Greenland icesheet. The Russians are flying a radar patrol to find out."

"Fine," said Sam sardonically, "if it isn't the Russians who bombed us!"

"French and British planes are flying in formation with them," Thale told him. "While you were gone I checked over what Communications has picked up. Everybody's cooperating. They have to! If whoever smashed us isn't smashed right back,

33

somebody else will be certain, presently, to get what we've had."

"Suppose the British or French planes found out it was the Russians and sent the news back?"

"If they did," Thale said, "the Russians would probably blow hell out of England or France before they were smashed. Oh, it's a bad business! Everybody's got to find out who did it, but it will take nerve to tell. I don't think it was the Russians, though. I can't think it was anybody, as far as that goes. The Burrows make the whole thing simply stupid. Nobody can conquer anybody with atomic bombs. They aren't fighting weapons. They aren't conquering weapons. They're just killing weapons. We didn't conquer Japan—just its government. You can't conquer anybody with bombs. They're not that sort of weapon!"

The loud-speaker muttered with the voices of radio amateurs.

"You're taking the short view," said Sam. "By the long view they're weapons of conquest, all right! Suppose we never find out who bombed us? Suppose that for months to come there are more bombs arriving, one by one, to smash our Burrows until none are left? What then?"

Thale shook his head, but Sam went on.

"The rest of the world is half-crazy, but afraid to start shooting for fear of killing its friends. Our enemy isn't afraid of killing its friends. It hasn't any. Its purpose will be to cause suspicion and destruction everywhere by any possible means. Including the use of bombs at explosive moments to get the Brienne Agreement invoked. Ultimately—"

Thale shrugged helplessly.

"Ultimately," said Sam savagely, "it will be the only nation with an industrial plant left, and it will have gotten most of the bombs in the world used up at one time or another. Most of the Burrows will be smashed, and it will probably know where the rest are. So one fine morning bombs will fall on the Burrows that do happen to be left, and then our enemy will simply march out its troops and casually start to rule what's left of the world. That's the point you miss, Fred. Atomic bombs can't conquer a nation. But they can conquer a world!"

"With luck," said Thale. "They'll need a lot of luck, though. And a lot of us will have to be unlucky. I'm going to make a point of not being that unlucky. I'm going to send at least one bomb against the people who did this."

The pneumatic message-tube popped loudly. Thale picked up the carrier and took out the form.

"Direct message from Sun Valley. Attachés from several consulates and a couple of Washington legations are there. Two of them have their wives along. They've agreed to come here if we send for them. Also a Major-General Thaddeus Warsaw. What the devil does an Army man want to come to a Burrow for?"

Sam shrugged.

"Somebody's picking off our Burrows one by one," he said bitterly, "and it's got to be stopped. Who's doing it? Somebody's got to find out so we can start sending bombs back. We'd better start to work on our guests!"

There was a tap on the door.

"Come in," said Sam.

The door opened. An orderly ushered in Betty Clarke.

"The lady, sir," he said formally, "says she has important news for the commanding officer, sir. The Personnel Officer told me to bring her here at once, sir."

With conflicting feelings, Sam stared at her, while he waited for Thale to take over. Here she was, as though in final confirmation of all the suspicions that he had tried to push down out of sight, during the days when he had seen so much of her. Yet there was a trace of the same stirring inside of him. For a moment he turned away, unable to look longer.

The girl's voice made him turn again.

"My brother and Steve and I located this Burrow. I thought we'd tell you how we did it. Unless you want a bomb to drop on it you'd better take a couple of safety measures."

She looked confidently from one to the other. But her hands gave her away. Her fingers worked nervously, twisting and knotting a little wisp of a handkerchief into a complicated form like a rosette, and then pulling it nervously apart, only to knot it again.

Sam made an inarticulate sound. He wanted to shout at her, to accuse her on the spot, and to drag from her by whatever means the whole story of her part in this vicious murder of a nation. But by sheer force he held on to himself and waited for Thale. The silence was insistent, dramatic. It became, through its intensity, a sound that filled the little room.

4

SOMEWHERE BEYOND THE STRATO-
sphere, where the sky was black and the stars were
unwinking specks of light and the moon was a monstrous disk whose ring-mountains were very clear
to see—somewhere above the dim dark bulk which
was the earth a rocket-bomb floated with a seemingly infinite leisureliness. Its propulsion-tubes no
longer jetted flames. It glowed brightly in the moon-
light. The shadows cast by its projecting parts were
almost savagely sharp. It was squat. It was ungainly.
It lacked the sleek smooth lines of a torpedo or even
the graceful catenary-curve taper of a long-range
artillery shell. It floated above a dark and feature-

less earth with no appearance of motion, no semblance of life.

But suddenly there were little puffings of vapor —instantly snatched away by the emptiness all about —and it turned in its floating. Its blunted, snout-like nose pointed downward. It floated on and on. Presently it wobbled a little. The infinitely thin outermost reaches of the atmosphere had touched it.

Later, the darkness which was the earth filled a larger part of the firmament. A long time later, there was a thin high screaming sound. The rocket-bomb was descending, almost imperceptibly, and the air grew thicker about it. It made, suddenly, a shrill small shriek. The shriek gained body and substance, but it was left behind. The rocket moved faster than the sound of its passage. It plunged down into the blackness which was earth, leaving in its wake a disembodied outcry that reached through miles and miles of thickening air, that followed down through cirrhus clouds of floating ice-particles five miles above the earth, and on still lower where the air was ever more dense.

The scream went wailing into the cold emptiness beneath the stars until, far below in the blackness,

39

there was a sudden flare of light brighter even than the sun at midday. It expanded with a terrible vehemence. In seconds it reached the stratosphere, and still it rose. It flung up a tumultuous mass of air like a prominence at the sun's limb. And presently out in emptiness, hundreds of miles high, the disappearance of the flare was followed by the formation of a thin mistiness that was frozen air and water-vapor from the cirrhus clouds that had been turned to steam, re-chilled by the cold of outer space and only very, very slowly settling back to earth.

On the ground, of course, there was merely a monstrous new chasm, like something gouged out by an unthinkable beast. The bomb had struck where there was dense forest on a mountain-flank. A mountain had ceased to be.

In the control-room of Burrow 89 the pneumatic tube popped loudly to break the silence, and Thale automatically plucked out the message. He said to Sam, without intonation, "Communications says Forty-One broke off communication in the middle of a message."

At last he turned to the girl. Looking at her impersonally, he said, "So you detected this Burrow and you want to tell us how you did it. Go ahead."

"We were mountain-climbing," the girl said steadily. "My brother Jerry, and Steve, and I. We were going to try to make the top of Mount Hanno. We stopped at a shelter-hut two-thirds of the way up to camp for the night. Jerry had a pocket radio. We were listening to a network program from New York when it stopped. Just like that. It stayed off. The Denver station we were tuned to apologized and said there was some trouble in New York. Until it was remedied they'd use records. Fifteen minutes later that station went off between two drum-beats. Jerry was puzzled. He tried for other stations. A lot of them seemed to be off the air. He was just tuning in on one, when it went off the way the Denver station had done. He kept trying, and trying, but the air seemed dead. Up on Mount Hanno we should have been able to receive anything, from any-where. . . ."

"You detected this Burrow, you say," said Sam with savage politeness. "How?"

The girl moistened her lips. For a moment he thought she was going to say outright, "Sam, why do you act that way?" But she didn't. She just kept on automatically twisting her handkerchief, and at last she turned again to Thale.

"Jerry switched to the amateur bands. They were all puzzled, wanting to know what was the matter. Some had been talking to other amateurs in one city or another, and they'd cut off. Some were saying the cross-country power lines had gone out and they'd had to shift to batteries. Then one of them pointed out that only small-town and rural stations were on the air. At last a voice said, 'Q R R! Q Ṙ R!' It was a terrible voice, somehow. The man said that atom bombs had fallen on the New York metropolitan district. He'd seen the flares, and though he was miles away they'd burned him. He'd felt the bomb-quakes. Houses had fallen down all around him, and fires were starting everywhere. He was dying, but he'd gotten his set to work so he could tell what had happened. And he said he was miles and miles from New York, but he was going to open his windows so we could hear what he heard. And we heard people screaming . . ." She added almost irrelevantly, "The fallen-down houses had caught fire."

Thale listened with an odd, absent-minded expression on his face. He glanced at the girl's nervous hands.

"You detected this Burrow—"

"M-mountain-climbing didn't seem very important," said the girl. "When dawn came we started back down. We tried to take a short-cut, for speed. And we got lost."

"You did," said Sam, unable to be quiet longer. "You got lost. . . ."

"We did!" insisted the girl. "And we—saw two figures on the snow. We shouted to them and they ran away. One of them shot at us. We—couldn't understand. We were scared, but we followed. Their tracks went out on a glacier—another glacier, not this one—and stopped suddenly."

Thale asked briefly, "Helicopter?"

"No. . . . It was a crevasse," said the girl. She swallowed. "Jerry went to the edge of it, with Steve and me braced against the ropes. He called down, but there wasn't any answer. They were gone. And we were lost, but we thought maybe they had friends or something; so we back-trailed them, and they'd dug in the snow. We looked and found where they'd dug to a sort of automatic radio transmitter. It was working, repeating signals it picked up with a micro-wave receiver."

Sam drew in his breath. With every word Betty

gave fresh proof that she was a spy. Because the Burrows, all of them, communicated with the outer world through a web of transmitting stations, all absolutely synchronous as to phase, and all remote-controlled from their parent Burrows because nobody has ever yet tapped a micro-wave beam. But even the main transmitters could not be found unless from very near, because the signal-strength of each one varied wildly. Very close, with a shielded loop, a transmitter might be located, but at a distance no direction-finder in the world could analyze the composite signal. Its apparent source changed constantly and insanely as the relative strength of the several transmitters changed. By phase-inversion of one or more, the signal could seem to come from a spot even outside the outermost of the transmitters. Its seeming source could travel hundreds of miles a second, and no locating instrument could pin it to any definite spot.*

"To be sure," Sam said with a deadly gentleness.

---

* "Quite right. There used to be two radio stations in Boston and Hartford with this phase relationship. A direction-finder very positively insisted that there was but one station, and that it was somewhere on a line between Boston and Hartford."—L. Jerome Stanton (in a personal letter to the author).

"You found one of our transmitters and tried to back-track its controlling beam. Only we don't send our controlling beams from the Burrow. Naturally! And you were away off even that course—"

"Jerry said we were miles south of the proper line," the girl admitted helplessly, "but we were going to try to get back on it and warn you—"

Thale broke in:

"It could be true, Sam. Send her off to Personnel for a screening process. I've got an idea."

Sam stood up.

"Come along," he said curtly.

The girl hesitated.

"If you—could," she said pleadingly, "would you —let my family know I'm all right? They live in Sacramento."

There was a sudden dead silence. Thale looked up. Sam felt something contract within him.

"I'm Betty Clarke," the girl explained, "and my family lives at 1170 Riverdale Road—"

She stared at the two of them. She had been pale before. Now every trace of color left her face.

"Has—please! Has anything—happened?"

"I'm afraid," said Sam," there's no use sending a message to Sacramento. A bomb fell on it."

The girl swayed. She looked blankly incredulous.

"I——think," she said, "that I'd like to sit down somewhere. . . ."

"In Personnel," replied Sam. "I'll help you there."

He took her arm. He led her out of the control-room. She walked like an automaton all the way, and neither of them spoke.

When he came back, Thale was talking into a transmitter. He broke the connection abruptly and switched off, while Sam paced bitterly up and down.

"I'm sending out the smaller helicopter," he observed. "I'm going to send that girl's brother with it. We'll see if we can find where two men dropped into a crevasse, and if we can we'll fish them out. If they were spies, there might be something on them that will tell whom they were working for."

"The girl's a spy herself," said Sam. "I know what I'm talking about, Thale."

Thale shrugged his shoulders.

"Possibly. But the trouble is that detection of a spy—even proof of it—isn't proof that that spy's nation is the one that bombed us. It's evidence, but not proof. Apparently you have a story to tell, Sam, but I'd rather wait till later to hear it."

He spoke with the detached precision that Sam

had noticed ever since Thale had recovered from the first shock of his personal loss.

"However," Thale added after a moment, "I think we might do something with a bomb, if we could get hold of one. It would take a hell of a lot of luck. . . . But we know their course, you know. Due south. If one came for us we'd know its target thirty seconds in advance. I'm going to talk to the Math officers and see how closely we could figure the trajectory of a bomb headed right here. We might send a bomb of our own to meet it, with a proximity fuse. Perhaps nothing at all would happen, but we might destroy it, or we might knock its gyros out, or—please God!—we might simply knock it down and track its fall with radar. No reason we shouldn't use radar if a bomb once comes for us. It's a long chance, though. I'll see what Math says. Take over here, Sam."

Sam Burton sat down in the commanding officer's chair and stared at nothing. The Burrows had been dug and built at a cost of millions to prevent attack by making vengeance for it certain. And now the attack had come and there was no vengeance; the Burrows and the men in them were useless. The feeling of impotence was the more horrible because every surviving human being in America craved vengeance even more than he craved continued life. Seventy million dead was not all the damage done by the bombs. Two hundred cities blasted was not the total destruction. The dead were dead. Vengeance could not bring them back. But those left alive were maimed.

Those who had been reared in cities and survived them were doubly struck. Not only had they lost families or friends. Their memories were crippled. It was no longer possible to remember anything of one's past without remembering also that it had ceased to exist. One's old home no longer existed. The streets, the parks, the schools, the soda-fountain of high-school years, the baseball lot, the gym where school dances were held and to which one took one's first date—these too were gone. The very substance of memory was destroyed. The effect was homesickness, acute and incurable. The most confirmed of misanthropes must hate this enemy who had destroyed the very substance of American life.

Sam Burton tried to prevent himself from thinking about the things that were crowding into his mind. But there was nothing to do in the control-room. If the detectors signaled a bomb on the way to this Burrow, there would be nothing to do but to grip the arms of one's chair and wait for annihilation. If nothing happened at all, there was still nothing to do. There were little relays over by the equipment-condition board on the far side of the room. They clicked on and off, and tiny electric lamps changed color. Those lamps indicated the condition and operation of every piece of machinery in the Burrow. Of them all the only significant ones —and even they had no meaning at present—were the dull-red glows that told of every launching-tube loaded and ready.

A light changed. The helicopter was on its way up the lift to its egress-port. Sam watched the light until the port light changed. He knew the helicopter was taking off, to swoop away through the night as it had done an hour since under his command. Its new errand was more gruesome. The heli would land, straddling a crevasse in a distant glacier, where two men had dropped presumably to their deaths. A winch and cable would lower other men into the narrowing icy crack, down into the very depths of a river of ice, surrounded by millions of tons of moving, shifting, transparent death, to seek for corpses.

But that was useless. Everything was useless. Save for spies—who would prove nothing—there could be no indication of the nation that had sent bombs upon America. The foreign radios were broadcasting protestations in many accents, offering help in vengeance, and food and medical supplies and sympathy—when their own cities were like knackers' stalls, filled with the dead victims of their own mass panics. And all the time one of those protesting nations had murdered the United States.

Sam Burton impotently shook his head. His own personal tragedy nagged at him. But he would not think of it. He fought to change the sense of loss to hatred. He sat still, staring at nothing.

The speaker by his elbow spoke abruptly. "Sam?"

"Yes," said Sam grimly. "What's up?"

"Math said," Thale's voice told him, "that the exact trajectory of a bomb headed for us would depend on the height it had been shot to. But the blast-effect of one of our own bombs ought to smash anything fairly close, and there couldn't be much variation of trajectory in the last thirty seconds with a given velocity, a given compass course, and a given target—from a long distance, of course. So I've put a proximity-fuse on one of our bombs. It'll go off if it passes close to an approaching one. It's loading up now in Tube Nine. It's set for a bomb coming due south to hit us. If the alarm-signal flashes, press the firing-button on Tube Nine."

"Right," said Sam. "Tube Nine. Anything else?"

"No. Signing off," said Thale's voice.

There was nothing to do. There was nothing at all to do. Bombs had fallen from empty space. As if in irony, they came from the North Pole, from the workshops of Santa Claus. The present from the North Pole this time had been death, and there was no way to return the gift. Nobody knew how many Burrows there were. In the lower levels of rank the estimate ranged from one hundred to two. But at any rate their launching-tubes could fling up into space—to fall anywhere on earth—such maniacal destruction as had not even been visited upon America. Yet now the Burrows must wait. Because they would not kill the wholly innocent, they waited, and waited, and waited and waited. . . .

The pneumatic tube popped loudly. Sam Burton reached over and plucked out the message. *"Number 93 no longer in communication. Believed knocked out."*

One by one, the Burrows themselves were in process of destruction. The nation they had believed they guarded was dead; its cities not even heaps of debris, but merely hollowed chasms in which poisonous radioactive gases formed and seeped out upon the countryside. The Burrows were useless, and doomed. The nation was a chaos of tiny, isolated hamlets and small towns, united only in their hatred of the unknown enemy. And in the Burrows there was the beginning of despair.

Sam Burton put his head in his hands. He would not think of the girl in Personnel. He would not think of despair. It was necessary that he stay sane and ready. The Burrows of America could almost destroy the civilization of the world. The temptation must be great, in every one of them, to let loose bombs on all the earth, to be sure of vengeance in a general holocaust.

At last, however, he gave up. He must think of Betty. It was the only way to keep insistent images of her from recurring to torment and distract him.

He had known her on his last leave. From the moment he had first seen her he had spent every possible minute with her. At the end of the first four days, he had admitted to himself that he was in love with her. Yet he was reluctant to admit it to Betty, to tell her outright. Not from any doubt that he did love her, but because of his growing uneasiness over her friends.

They had been too cordial to him. They had wined and flattered him, and he felt uneasily that they tried to pump him. There could be, he knew, only one reason to ask questions about the Burrows. A loyal citizen wouldn't want to know these secrets. Only spies would fish for information about the nation's only defense against what had happened. So Sam had left, uncertain and unhappy, without telling Betty what he wanted to tell her. Yet he hadn't reported her friends as suspicious persons. He had told himself he wasn't sure enough.

And now—now she was here, as though in confirmation of his worst fears. As though to confront him with his own guilt—

A gong rang violently. Its sound was like a blow, and Sam's heart made a leap in his breast. It hurt. A light glowed luridly blue-white. The alarm-signal. A bomb headed here. . . .

He jammed his thumb down savagely upon the firing-button of Tube Nine. Then he gripped the arms of his chair and waited for death.

Far down in the bowels of the earth there was a

roaring. It was a rocket-bomb going up the launch-ing-tube. Actually, by the time the sound reached his ears, the bomb was out and climbing furiously for the stars. But he heard it as a long-drawn-out roar.

"Whooo-oooo-OOOO-OOOO-OOOOMMMM!"

Then it was gone. There was silence. A clock ticked loudly. Sweat stood out on Sam's face. His eyes savage, he waited for annihilation. . . .

5

*A*T SIXTY SECONDS AFTER THE RINGING
of the alarm gong, he heard a dull, rumbling whis-
per. There was a faint vibration in the earth. There
was a murmuring. That was all.

Then the pneumatic tube at Sam's elbow popped
loudly. He opened the message-carrier with shak-
ing fingers. The curled-up yellow slip within said,
*"Atomic flare seen in stratosphere due north very
close."* Sam swallowed. He reflected rather absurdly
that he might be dead, that perhaps this was what
came after death—that one wasn't aware of any particular change, at first. But he threw a switch to
Communications and said:

55

"Put this in top-secret code and send to all Burrows. Message follows: 'Report successful interception of enemy bomb by one of ours, using calculations of necessary trajectory assuming enemy bomb crossed North Pole headed due south. Proximity fuse was apparently effective within margin of error of calculation at meeting-point of our bomb and enemy's. Urge immediate adoption this device by all Burrows.' Message ends."

He wiped sweat from his face. It had been a fluke. Not altogether, to be sure, but there was a large element of luck in it. You can't intercept an artillery shell, still less a rocket-bomb traveling at four miles a second. Actually, they hadn't hit the enemy rocket. That was inconceivable. But they had mined the avenue by which it must approach. They'd sent up a rocket of their own, accelerating swiftly, but still crawling by comparison with the enemy projectile. Their rocket had a proximity fuse—a fuse that caused it to detonate by coming into the mere neighborhood of another solid object, as a magnetic mine in the Second World War was set off by the mere nearness of a ship. Their bomb had been set off by the approach of the other. But the trick had worked only because they'd known the direction and very nearly the angle at which the enemy bomb must arrive. Even then it was very largely luck.

Sam threw the General Communication switch and announced, "We just safely detonated a bomb coming for us, far away. You can howl if you like, but there'll be others. I repeat, we just detonated an enemy bomb coming for us."

He was not elated. As a matter of fact, he felt sick. The location of Burrow 89 was plainly, now, known to the enemy. There would be more bombs coming. They might come in flights of twos or threes or dozens, at half-second or quarter-second intervals. Undoubtedly they would no longer come from the North Pole. If bombs could be sent to the Pole to change their course there and come on as if the Pole had been their launching-site, they could be sent to other places.

But if he was not elated, others were. His words had been heard in every cubbyhole of the Burrow. He heard a thin ullulation in the corridors. The garrison of Burrow 89 was rejoicing. Not at its own safety—that was gone—but at the triumph of having cheated even one enemy bomb of its prey. Of course more bombs could come from every quarter of the compass, in twos and fours and dozens. . . .

Still, there was a chance that if they did come from a new direction they might be spotted on the way, and that by the time Eighty-Nine was destroyed, the other Burrows might be closer to the trail of the enemy.

The door opened and Thale came in again. His eyes were beginning to glow a little, but his face was still strained and taut.

"We're adapting some other rockets for interceptors," he said, "and we're setting up radars of our own. No reason we shouldn't, since they know our position. We're also setting up snapper-bomb batteries. The radars are going to feed into course-computers for the snapper-bombs* and fire them automatically. They'll save two or three seconds that way, and snapper-bombs can make a lot of use of that!"

"No harm in trying," said Sam.

"According to the Army radars, though," Thale went on, "the enemy bomb either detonated or was vaporized. I was hoping just to knock one down. If we could get a good look at an enemy job . . ."

* The Mark XI Counter-Attack Rocket was equipped with a minute radar which guided it to its target, and had a proximity fuse to detonate it nearby. It was called a "snapper-bomb" because of its extreme acceleration. When fired it seemed simply to snap out of sight.

"I'd like to get a good look at a rocket course on its way to the North Pole," said Sam grimly.

"The Army's had bombers flying over the Pole for four hours now, trying to spot them. Nothing yet, though. Probably too high. But finding out where they come from won't solve our whole problem, Sam. Our enemy's certainly not sending bombs from its own territory. It would be some place in Greenland or in the mid-Pacific. If we found it and didn't blast it beyond identification, it could blast itself in case of need. Tough job, Sam!"

Sam changed the subject abruptly.

"It looks like the people we picked up are spies, all right!"

"It's not proved," said Thale, with quiet precision. "There's evidence, but no proof. You can't see that. You're all wrought up, Sam."

"Why not?" Sam demanded. "It took them an hour and twenty-five minutes to bomb Centralia—and they had to figure a trajectory. How long before they send some more bombs after us?"

"Do you expect me to worry about that?" asked Thale, smiling faintly. "Clear out, Sam!"

Sam shrugged his shoulders and rose.

"I'll go poking around," he growled. "I figure

that next time they'll send a flock of bombs at us from different directions, and they'll get us. So I might as well be unpleasant while I'm alive."

He went out of the control-room. His feeling of futility had not lessened in the least. The only thing that would ease it would be to hear the "Whoo-ooo-OOOO-OOOOO-OOOOMMM!" of bombs going out the launching-tube with a real target at the end of their flight. He longed for vengeance—not simply for vengeance's sake, but to re-establish in a torn and despairing world the idea of justice and hope. Not only the United States had been murdered, but all that man held it good to live for, as well. The very concepts of justice and hope must be sown again, planted anew with infinite care. And if this assassination went unpunished, the sowing would be impossible.

Sam looked down and saw his hands clenched tightly. By force of will he relaxed them. Thale could say calmly that they had no proof—but that didn't mean that it was impossible to get proof. Betty could do no more harm; but she might unwittingly do good. She might—he hesitated at the fierceness of his feeling—she might be forced to do good. If knowledge of certain death ahead unnerved her, she might let slip something that would be useful if passed on to the Burrows that would survive this one. . . .

She had cried a little, but she was composed when he found her in Personnel. There were two Wacs with her, both wearing the half-stunned expression characteristic of survivors. They went out when Sam scowled at them.

Sam stared at her.

"You know we knocked down a bomb aimed for us?" he asked slowly, continuing to stare with deliberate harshness.

She replied steadily, "I—heard you announce it over the speaker system."

"I should have paid you a tribute then," he told her. "You tipped them our position. When you were on the glacier we listened to you with everything we had, but we couldn't detect a signal. How'd you do it? A microwave beam? How'd you aim it?" He made his voice as personally scornful as he could.

She looked directly at him.

"I'm not a spy, Sam, but it would be a waste of time to insist on it." Her voice was suddenly tired. "You're determined to believe I am. Some day you'll know the truth. If you don't believe me now, why bother?" Then she said, "How's Steve? He hurt his leg pretty badly."

"He's in the infirmary," Sam told her, "under truth-serums and scopolamine and such things—" he regarded her narrowly— "while our psychological officer asks questions in a friendly voice and in different languages. *And* watches certain instruments. He'll get the facts, even though we don't use torture. Quaint of us not to use torture, isn't it?"

"He'll be all right," Betty replied quietly, "if it's only facts you want."

"You'll be dead shortly," said Sam coldly. "So will all of us for that matter. There'll be more bombs coming along that we're not likely to handle. So it wouldn't do any harm to admit that you're a spy."

She said nothing.

"You might even," he told her ironically, "make us believe you're working for one nation when it's another that bombed us. That would be a service to your country."

Her voice was very quiet now.

"Perhaps you think I should have gotten hysterical when I heard Sacramento was wiped out. Is that it?"

He shrugged his shoulders, but his eyes—hot and angry—did not leave her face.

She went on evenly, "I could explain, but you—wouldn't believe me. You wouldn't believe anything I told you." Her voice finally broke and then rose defiantly. "Why should I try to explain that I'm holding on with both hands to what self-control I've got?"

He forced himself not to change expression or tone.

"There's no reason whatever to explain it," he said. "I'm not interested. But if you're worried for fear your companions have cracked, your brother's out in the helicopter. He agreed to show us where you claim two men dropped into a crevasse. We're going to fish for them."

There was not even a flash of alarm in her eyes. She looked at him with resolute composure.

"You've got half an hour or less to live." Sam's voice was suddenly harsh in his own ears, and the sound increased his anger. "And I've got half an hour to live. Because of you. And you're feeling pretty smug because you think we're such softies that we won't torture the truth out of you! There's just a chance you're wrong."

She swallowed.

"Sam. Look at me. Maybe we—will all be killed. But that makes everything look rather puny, doesn't it? Why do you hate me so? It isn't really just that you think I'm a spy. I know it isn't. Something—something's collapsed in you."

He stared at her, anger rising again—and something besides anger. She reached out and touched his arm.

"My—mother and father are dead, Sam. Killed in the bombing. And it—looks like I'm going to be dead soon, too. You tell me so, anyhow—that we both are. Well, I'd like to die on my feet. And I would have thought you would too. And—if I could I'd like it to be with someone I—with someone who was angry enough and strong enough to help me keep on my feet and fighting. Is that too much to ask?"

"Meaning me?"

"Why not? I'd be too proud to weaken where you could see me, Sam. And I'd like not to weaken."

He laughed. He wasn't amused, but he was checkmated. He didn't know what he believed any more.

"All right! I'll take you up on that," he said finally. "I'm off duty. Come along. I'll show you some of the people who'll die with you. I said *with* you."

He led the way to the door. They would perhaps live a few minutes. The enemy knew the location of Eighty-Nine, and could send over bombs in some combination that counter-bombs couldn't handle—not even the snapper-bombs with their rocket acceleration of a hundred gravities and bomb-load of half a ton of chemical explosive. Defense against rocket bombs at four miles a second simply wasn't practical. The Burrow would do what it could, but it would be a losing fight from the beginning. To show her the Burrow could do no harm. And it might hurt. He wanted to hurt her. That was all he was sure of—he still wanted to hurt her.

"I'll show you around," he told her. "It may be amusing to see all the things your principals would like to know, even though they won't ever learn them from you."

She came composedly with him. He led the way out of Personnel.

"Personnel, where you were," he told her in the corridor outside, "takes care of records and pay and all that, but also it handles psych tests—screenings for people with tendencies to crack up. It's somewhat trying on the nerves to live underground for months on end. Until the bombs fell, only the top officers knew where this Burrow was actually located. There were very intricate tricks for keeping the rest of us from knowing where we were going when we came here. When the war started, Thale and I opened up the top-secret safe and got our positions, then unlocked the surface televisions and took a look around. Quaint to see the out-of-doors for the first time in a couple of months."

She listened. He went on, "There's Math, where they plot trajectories. Want to look in?"

She shook her head. He moved on, walking with jerky strides.

"Thale wasn't Burrow Commander, and I wasn't adjutant, but things looked quiet. Our CO and adjutant—in fact, the top four officers—went to Washington to urge a new gadget somebody had dreamed up. Thale and I were left in charge, and a bomb fell on Washington. Wonderful timing, your friends! They got our top Army and Navy commanders; they bagged the President and all the cabinet but the Secretary of Agriculture; they got about everybody in forty minutes. And they've been knocking off Burrows ever since."

—There was a deep-toned roar from the very bowels of the earth. *"Whoooo-ooooo-OOOOO-*

OOOOO-OOOOOMMMM!!!" It was distinctively and unmistakably the roar of a rocket going up the launching-tube. The noise stopped. The rocket was on its way toward the stars.

"That's it," said Sam. "Our detectors must have spotted a bomb coming here. We sent out an interceptor. Not snapper-bombs yet—no time. It won't work. We've got maybe twenty seconds."

She went a little bit paler, but she stood steadily facing him.

"Come on!" he said bitterly. "Why not tell me the truth now? Fifteen seconds to go."

"I'm not a spy," she said. She was white and frightened, but she held tight to her self-control. She looked suddenly, infinitely pathetic.

Sam put his arm about her in a futile gesture of protectiveness. She looked up at him briefly, tense with the expectation of death. Utterly without premeditation, he kissed her. And even at this moment her eyes widened.

"It won't hurt," he said gruffly.

She glanced up again. They braced themselves and waited.

And nothing happened.

6

THE GLACIER WOUND AND TWISTED BE-
tween upthrust walls of naked stone. Mountain peaks
yearned toward the stars. The curving, tortured surface of the ice-river gave out from time to time
groaning and clashing sounds—sudden yieldings of
ice or stone to the frozen motion of the stream. The
ice which lay above Burrow 89 had been white snow
a thousand years ago, new-fallen on the mountain-
tops. The white snowbanks now lying on the distant
mountains would be ice a thousand years from now,
and moving with an invincible deliberation toward
the valleys down below.

There was the feeling of eternity among the mountains; of a vast, vast patience and of a tranquillity which ignored the doings of men. The high hills could afford to disregard man. He was a newcomer, an ephemerid, who only yesterday wore hides and painted his red skin and avoided the mountains out of terror, and only a little while since had dared to fly above them in clumsy things contrived of metal. He had never yet appeared in numbers on the snow-fields.

Now, however, there were stirrings at this spot and that. Like an anthill at the time of the queen ants' flight, new openings appeared at unexpected spots. Furred figures hurried out of the openings and were frantically busy with ridiculous activities. Lights appeared—sharply glaring electric lights— which could be seen for miles. Men came swarming up from underground and labored frenziedly on the surface.

But, deep down in the Burrow, Sam Burton flicked off the switch of a communicator with which he had called Thale in the control-room. He drew a long breath, and said slowly, "We sent a bomb to Greenland, by request. The Russian radar-planes spotted something there. They weren't sure, but it was suspicious. So we bombed it. This is the only Burrow we are sure the enemy has located without annihilating, so we might as well use our launching-tubes. No use in another Burrow's exposing itself when spies may not have found it. That's why we were elected. I hope we killed somebody!"

Betty looked at him steadily.

"We'll continue our tour," said Sam abruptly, turning away. "No point in it, of course, but there's no point in anything—except getting even with the crowd that's smashed us. We'll go down this ramp. Recreation rooms and so on."

They went down the sloping corridor and there were the rooms in which the garrison of Burrow 89 amused itself. There were game rooms and a swimming pool and a tennis court—a high-ceilinged cavern lit by fluorescent lamps a thousand feet under the ice of Rainier Glacier—and there was a miniature television theatre and a somewhat larger motion picture theatre with a poster announcing a picture to be shown at "1600 hours Burrow Time." Then there was a corridor of shops—not canteens—with window displays calculated to appeal to the Wacs of the garrison, and beyond that a gardening area in which the smell of green things was oddly incongruous with the rocky ceiling and the glaring white lamps that were substituted for daylight.

"The lights are regulated to simulate the hours of daylight at different seasons of the year," Sam continued in his guide's voice, "so that we can make any kind of plants or vegetables bloom at any time of year we want. This garden's for recreation, though. We grow our food lower down still, in hydroponic tanks."

He still could not look directly at her.

"It looks," said Betty thoughtfully, "as if the Burrows mean that people could keep on living even if a new ice age came."

"What? Oh, yes," Sam replied listlessly. "If there were any point in it. We'll see the hydroponic gardens on the next lower level."

He led the way down a long, sloping tunnel which curved and curved again. In all its length it was lighted by glaring tubes of white light. Power was the one thing of which the Burrow had a plethora. The more power that was used, the more atomic explosive could be put in store, and the Burrows were not only forts but arsenals for the manufacture of the weapons that the world had depended on for the preservation of peace.

"You can smell the plants," Sam went on without interest as they went down and down. "Among other things, they use up the carbon dioxide in the air and help the air-purifiers in that way. They help with the air-moistening problem, too. We wouldn't want to be pumping air in and out all the time. It would show up on a thermal-detector screen like a house on fire."

He opened a door. There was the sound of rippling water. There were rows and rows of lights—the white actinic light of fluorescence, and the bluish glare of non-fluorescent tubes which let out their ultra-violet light unchanged. There were banks and banks of troughs, from which the rippling sounds came, and there were plants growing within them with a rankness and luxuriance inconceivable in nature. The air was filled with the smell of green stuff and the curious cool fresh smell of running water, and there were a myriad faint odors ranging from the pungent tang of tomato-plants to the quaint thin odor of squash-blossoms.

"Here we are," said Sam. "Air purification, food supply, vitamins—everything all in one. We let the stuff run to leaves because it helps the air. Actually we grow more than we can eat, right here."

The hydroponic garden seemed to cover acres. There were separate caverns in which different hours of "daylight" could be observed, but there were wide archways in between, so that as the sloping ramp reached floor level one could see on and on along the troughs in which plants grew more lushly than in tropical jungles.

"Seen enough?" asked Sam. "Or do you want to go on and see the rest?"

"Where are all the people?" she asked, ignoring his question. "It's empty!"

"Most people are on the surface," Sam replied. "The first defense of a Burrow is secrecy. Our secrecy is gone. So the garrison's up on the surface frantically setting up radars and snapper-bomb emplacements for a second line. They're setting up Johnson detectors and infra-red gadgets. They all boiled out of the recreation-rooms and every place but Math and the can-room down below. Want to see that?"

Her eyes widened.

"Can-room?"

"Our bombs," he told her without smiling, "are officially called Self-Propelled Atomic Missiles. So of course in ordinary speech they're SPAM. And the tubes they're put in are cans. Cans for SPAM. Can-room. The rocket-launching chamber."

When they had gone through another door, they faced elevators. He pressed a button. Almost instantly an elevator came to a cushioned stop and its door opened. The elevator was empty. He ushered her in and closed the door. He pressed a button within. Nothing happened.

Then a voice spoke from the ceiling, with the tinny quality of a small-sized loud-speaker.

"Lieutenant, sir," said the voice, *"I recognize you all right, but the lady—"*

"She's a spy," said Sam in a level voice. "One of the three I brought in with the helicopter. Check with Major Thale, if you like."

"Yes, sir."

There was a pause. The elevator descended slowly. After seconds, it abruptly increased its downward speed. Sam grinned.

"Television unit. He checked," he told the girl. "We're rather careful about the can-room. Don't move suddenly down there, by the way. You'll be watched every second."

The elevator slowed and stopped. Its door opened,

and they stepped into a completely closed room. After a moment one of the doors opened.

"They checked still again," Sam explained drily. "A little way down here, and you'll see as much as you're ever likely to."

She paused uncertainly, and then followed him down a corridor. Seconds later they stood in a dome-roofed room a hundred feet across and more than a hundred feet high. Its ceiling was naked, seamless stone. Its floor was a whitish, soft, resilient stuff that gave slightly under one's feet. There was no furniture except a round table in the middle, on which a pitiless white light shone. The outstanding architectural feature of the room was certain giant pipes which emerged from the rocky wall some fifty feet up and slanted slightly inward so that at the floor level they were completely inside. Tall, twenty-foot rounded doors completed their tube-shape at their bottom ends. There was a large round metallic disk in the floor before each, and a gleaming robot-like mass of shining metal beside every one.

"These," said Sam with irony, "these are our jewels. They are the launching-tubes the Burrows were built to house. Each one has a bomb in it, fueled to hit any spot on earth we set it for. The trajectory-control is that complicated gadget alongside. That's worked from Math. From all the way up top, they can set the controlling machinery inside the bomb to make it take any path they please, change course wherever they please, and come down where they want it to. This Burrow has been in existence for twelve years. It cost forty million dollars—and cheap at that. It houses nine hundred men and women to service these tubes, and so far it's only fired two shots. One knocked off an enemy bomb by a fluke, one dropped—no, will drop presently—on a suspicious spot on the Greenland ice-sheet. And if that was a launching-site, it's turned to vapor and we'll never know who was in it!"

There were men in this place, but they were almost unnoticeable at first. Then one of the tube side-doors swung back abruptly, disclosing the monstrous torpedo-shape of the rocket-bomb within. Men moved swiftly about it. There were surprisingly many. The bomb came out of the tube, and swung to one side. It looked long and sleek and horrible, but somehow it was distinctively an American product. No one could look at it and think of it as made anywhere but in the United States. It was somehow terrifying to see in an instrument of such destructiveness a family likeness to American automobiles and iceboxes and transport planes and radios and cigarette lighters and electric stoves. It was impossible to put a finger on that likeness, but if you looked at it you knew its nationality.

The metal disk in the floor rose. It went up and up and up—and there was another bomb, equally huge and deadly and beautiful in its trimness. It swung into the emptied tube. The door closed. A light glowed somewhere. Then a buzzer sounded.

There was a bellowing within the tube and then a roaring noise. But here, at the spot from which the bomb departed, the sound of its going was strange. Its pitch went down and down to inaudibility, until it was merely a powerful throbbing in the air, as its speed approached that of sound and then exceeded it.

It was gone. Sam moved toward the group about the tube. A sergeant came quickly to meet him. Sam talked in a low tone while there was a whistling of compressed air, and then the tall door reopened. The tube was empty, and the bomb which had been removed was replaced in it. Sam went back to Betty.

"The British, operating out of Singapore, got some weird radar-indications out in mid-Pacific. They might have been from a bomb launched from a sub out there. And again we're the only Burrow whose location is known to the enemy that we're sure of, and hence the only one which might as well use up its rockets before it's smashed. So we heaved a bomb over there—a straight detonation bomb with no radar or other fancy attachments. An atomic bomb," he added, "is a very, very effective depth-bomb. But if we smashed what the bombs are coming from, we'll never know who sent them."

She smiled again.

"Don't you think you're telling me too much? Suppose a miracle happened and we were not killed? Think what I know and can tell my mythical country."

"I'm not worried about that," he said. "Miracles don't come in dozens—and that's what we'd need."

He started to say something more—something impulsive. But he stopped himself, and led the way back to the small bank of elevators. One stood open. He took her inside, closed the door, and pushed the button. It began to rise swiftly. He looked down at her and again opened his lips to speak, but once more refrained. There was a television unit within the car, and microphones for the inspection and questioning of passengers before they neared the can-room where the launching-tubes ended and the Burrow's bombs were fired.

The elevator rose silently, but there was suddenly a rumbling, crashing sound—the dull concussion of chemical explosions somewhere. They came in a frantic, unrhythmic succession. All were dull. All were muffled. All came from somewhere overhead.

"Snapper-bombs taking off," he remarked grimly. "Another bomb or a flock of them has been radar-spotted coming for us. Somebody, maybe ten thous-and miles away, sent some bombs at us maybe half or three-quarters of an hour ago. So we're fighting. You're in a battle. We've still no idea whom we're fighting, and they can have no notion of how or even whether we're fighting back. This is atomic war. In a couple of seconds more we'll find out the answer —for us."

7

A MOUNTAIN FLANK—SERENE BENEATH the stars—with wide slopes of stone on which snow lay irregularly, suddenly sputtered in an insane fashion. Small explosive sparks flashed upon the rocky spaces, or glared briefly upon surrounding areas of snow. From each spark another spark shot skyward with incredible, almost lunatic, velocity. At first the ascending sparks seemed silent, but presently the sounds of their going echoed among the mountains. They were wabbling, high-pitched wailing noises which moved about in emptiness, lost from the things that had made them.

There had been twenty or thirty sparks upon the

mountain; there were as many disembodied wailings wandering among the hills. And, miles high above the earth, twenty or thirty small objects hurtled skyward with ever-increasing speed. They did not float upward, like projectiles. They drove upward with a furious energy. Instant by instant their speed increased at an acceleration rate of one hundred gravities. This was only one two-hundredth that of an artillery shell in the bore of a cannon, which increases its speed twenty thousand times faster than gravitational acceleration, but a shell accelerates for only the fiftieth of a second and coasts the rest of its flight. These objects possessed rocket-tubes which flared a terrible quiet flame, and in their first second's flight they had risen three thousand two hundred feet: in their next second of flight their speed rose to six thousand four hundred feet per second. Five seconds after they took off they were seven and a half miles high and raging on at three miles per second.

They traveled in a cluster, like a tiny group of meteors. Some were ahead of the rest, and some were behind, and some were to the right and some to the left. Their drive-flames suddenly winked out in swift, irregular succession. In the fraction of a second they all went hurtling onward seemingly inert. But they moved at three miles per second. They spread out and filled a larger area of space. They ceased to seem like a close-knit group of meteors. They resembled rather a lonely group of dead or dying stars.

The earth was blackness below. The group of snapper-bombs was eighteen miles up only ten seconds after its departure. It formed an irregular globular cluster more than a mile in diameter, which still expanded.

At twelve seconds a drive-flame flared again. Then two flames. Then a dozen. All. The snapper-bombs began to weave about in erratic, unpredictable patterns, changing course with a frantic haste. Tiny radars in their make-up had detected something very far ahead. They controlled the snapper-bombs' drive jets to force them in its path. Invariably they overcorrected, so that the bombs darted recklessly over and over and over again into collision-courses along the line the approaching object would follow.

The nearing thing was ungainly; a clumsy, hideous thing of alien outward design. It plunged heavily toward earth at a velocity of four miles per second. The snapper-bombs came weaving crazily to meet it at three miles per second.

The foremost snapper-bomb missed. It passed astern. The second and third and fourth. . . . But then—too fast for any human eye to follow—the falling thing was englobed. No snapper bomb actually touched it. At a relative speed of seven miles a second, such a thing was inconceivable. But a snapper went off almost at the nose of the falling thing. Another detonated to one side. Above, below, before, behind. . . . Chemical explosions flared brightly—

But not for long. They became very puny, trivial, in the awful radiance which burst from the atomic bomb. It filled the sky and seemed to envelope the universe. It was brighter than the surface of the sun. Its temperature was hundreds of thousands or millions of degrees. Some of the snapper-bombs were engulfed and vaporized in it, and the setting-off of mere half-tons of chemical explosive was undetectable in the monstrous detonation of an atomic bomb some forty-odd miles above the earth.

But a few of them were not engulfed, because they were beyond it and flashing away from the detonation at seven miles per second. They went on and on and out from earth—and very briefly afterward their drive-flames flashed again and they wove crazily and closed upon a second ungainly thing—and there was a second atomic explosion sixty miles up from earth before the radiance from the first had died.

Deep down under the glacier which had glinted so brightly in the two great flares, Sam Burton went into the control-room of Burrow 89 with Betty Clarke beside him. It was perhaps two minutes after the snapper-bombs took off. Thale sat in the commander's chair, his shoulders sagging, his eyes fixed on a television screen which showed the sky above. There were bright stars showing as tiny specks. Now and again—rarely—the tiny trail of a shooting star streaked across some portion of the screen.

"H'llo, Sam," said Thale quietly. "We didn't do it."

"We didn't do what?"

"We didn't knock down a bomb, as I had hoped—so that we could look at its works," said Thale heavily. "They sent two bombs at us this time. We got them both. You know, the funny thing is that they're still coming due south. You'd think they'd have changed that."

Sam sat down. He did not look at Betty, but he

could feel her presence close to him. With difficulty he pinned himself down to the problem at hand.

"Here's a possibility," he said. "Every nation on earth has its radars out and working. Everybody's trying to find out who's sending the bombs and from where, and nobody's succeeding. I've got an idea. It doesn't take twice as much fuel to send a rocket twice as far, when you get up into thousands of miles, because the landing-point is below the horizon and it has farther to fall before it lands. When you shoot at something beyond the horizon, you're shooting downhill."

Thale nodded.

"If you can send a rocket six thousand miles," said Sam, "you can practically send it around the earth. Hardly any more fuel needed, anyhow."

"True enough," Thale agreed. "But—"

"We haven't been figuring on that," said Sam. "Look! Every radar on earth is working, or pretending to. But radars work in straight lines. Their beams don't curve. Even so, most of the world is pretty well covered. In Europe, with national boundaries rambling every which way, radar-beams definitely overlap. The bombs aren't coming from Europe. Switzerland, for instance, couldn't send up bombs without the French or Spanish or Italians detecting them on the way up. One can rule out Finland and Sweden for the same reason. Radar-beams from neighboring countries meet overhead like the beams of a sloping roof. But—well—out in the mid-Pacific radar installations are far apart. Their beams—if they have range enough—will meet away out in space. They make a roof that's genuinely high. Bombs could be sent up and keep under that roof until they reached the Arctic. There are places in Asia where the same thing could be done. And of course Russia. . . ."

"Russia ought to be out," Thale interrupted him, "because it's the one nation the greatest number of people would be first to suspect. Whoever bombed us is in danger enough. Russia would be in more danger than most. They'd be fools to try it. Besides, Russia's opened up its air to planes of all nations, requiring only that planes of at least three other nations fly together, so that no one can report something that isn't so. That makes sense. Russia doesn't want to get wiped out by the rest of the world, and if our enemy isn't Russia, Russia may be next on the list."

"But I'm not thinking of Russia as a site for launching the bombs," Sam went on. "There's another place so vastly much better. Antarctica, Fred. There's a continent where nobody lives. Build a Burrow there and stock it with bombs and it would be pretty safe. The bombs could go up the Pacific, change course at the North Pole, and come on from there. About six thousand miles. Distance doesn't matter much as far as fuel goes."

Thale was suddenly still. Then he nodded.

"That," he said softly," is an idea. I'll spread that through the other Burrows, Sam. But not abroad. It didn't occur to me before, Sam, but once you do think of it there are certain obvious measures. . . ." His features tightened. "Of course the difficulty is that if there are bases in Antarctica, and if we bomb them, we're likely not to find out who built and manned them. And we've got to find that out!"

"I've thought of something else," Sam said. "Does it occur to you that the Perseids are about due? Any hour now. What will they do to our detectors?"

Thale shrugged.

"We—this Burrow—are using radar now, and they'll register. But their velocities will be wrong and their temperatures too low. Infra-red scanners will spot them, and Johnston detectors will pick 'em out every time too.* They're a complication, but we can't hope for simplicity yet. That's why I want to knock down a bomb and look at its works." He added, "The helicopter we sent to fish in the crevasse found one man down there. Dead, of course. They're bringing him back for a lookover." Then he glanced at the girl. "Her brother's on board. They got banged about a bit by the bombs. They made quite a concussion-wave on the surface. They should be back any time now."

"I'll take her over to meet it," said Sam, "unless you want me on duty."

Thale shook his head.

"I'd rather stick around here."

In silence, Sam got up and opened the door for the girl. They went out. Sam led the way in silence toward the lift going up to the helicopter egress-port.

---

* Johnson detectors and infra-red scanners, both depending on radiations originating in distant objects, and with those radiations governed by the object's temperature, give indications which vary with the temperature of the object. Therefore they will sort out very cold objects at the temperature of interplanetary space from objects which have been in airless space for a relatively short time and were, moreover, heated in their upward passage through the atmosphere. Radar gives no indication of temperature, but gives excellent readings of velocity.

"What are the Perseids?" she asked, after a moment. "I know—the meteor-shower. They're the August meteors, aren't they?"

"Right," Sam replied. "The earth crosses a comet's orbit, which always has meteors barging around in it. So for three days the number of shooting stars goes away up. And since radars are always picking up meteors anyhow, it means that our radar screens will be crowded with meteor trails and it'll be harder to distinguish bombs."

"But—"

"Meteors are faster," he explained. "Seven miles a second, and up to fifty. Their temperature is different. The detectors will sort them out, but it takes time and we haven't any time to spare." He added awkwardly, "By the way, it's not likely anybody in the helicopter was hurt by radiation from the bombs that've been set off. They went off away up where there was practically no air. Practically no secondary radiation. That's what does a lot of damage."

She was silent a moment. They went through a doorway and traveled another long corridor. Suddenly she spoke again.

"Sam, when we used to know each other, why did you suddenly just—vanish? We hadn't quarreled."

He drew a long breath.

"Your friends," he said heavily. "Look here, Betty. You know. They made too much over me. They tried a little too hard to get me drunk. Some of the girls almost threw themselves at my head. All very brightly and amusingly and cleverly—but too brightly and amusingly and cleverly. You know that."

She nodded slowly.

"Yes. I know—what you mean."

He hurried on.

"I was in the Atomic Service, remember, and on leave. And the Service was pretty important to me. I believed, like all of us, that we were the Service that really protected the United States. The men in the Service are pretty carefully picked. Most of them have families. A lot of them have traditions of generations of Army and Navy service."

She looked puzzled, but waited for him to go on.

"But I had nothing like that," said Sam in an even tone. "I have no family, and there was nobody on earth to be disgraced if I made a fool of myself. So I was being trusted more than most when they gave me a commission in the Atomic Service. It sounds stuffy, maybe, but I—took it pretty seriously."

Betty impulsively put her hand on his arm. He went doggedly on.

"So I met you. And I fell for you. I fell hard. I'm not a praying sort of person, but I—felt very much like getting down on my knees and thanking God because—well, He'd made you."

She was silent.

"At first I was pretty blind," he told her steadily. "You and your friends. . . . Such cordiality to a junior officer in the Atomic Service! Such charm! Such hospitality! And you—" He stopped. "It wasn't until one of your friends got a little too cordial and practically tipped his hand that I realized that every damned one of them was a bit on the shady side. Then I began to notice. You'll be amused to know that my first thought was to make sure and then tell you; so you'd drop them. I did make sure. I pretended to have gotten just drunk enough to be loose-tongued. And they pumped me. Delicately. Cleverly. Not in a fashion to arouse the suspicions of a slightly tipsy junior officer. Not even in a fashion which, testified to in court, would have convicted them as spies. But they pumped me."

She looked at him steadily.

"Go on."

"I was going to tell you what I'd found out. But suddenly I realized that you were pumping me too. You were asking me questions which seemed to be the sort that came from absorbed personal interest in me. But they weren't. I didn't know where my Burrow was? But how did I get there? How long did it take? Somebody must know the location. I must know north and south! And didn't room-radios with built-in loop antennas have to be turned around to get different stations? **You got quite technical, Betty."**

"I—" Then she stopped, helplessly.

"So I ducked out," he said without emotion. "I haven't had much fun, since. I've persuaded myself a dozen times over that I was all wrong and you were all right. I've told myself that I was a fool—that you were beginning to care for me, and that I spoiled it all by being suspicious. But then I picked you up off a glacier, trying to find this Burrow for whoever has murdered a good many millions of fairly innocent people. That was what I had to believe when I found you, after all that had gone before."

He looked down. There were tears in her eyes.

"And now?" she asked.

"Here's the lift," he said carefully. "The helicopter's coming down now."

They stood in a cavern with drill-marked walls, large enough to house a dozen aircraft. At one end a polished, rounded, oily shaft rose from the center of a shallow pit below an orifice going indefinitely upward from the roof. The metal shaft was descending now, sliding smoothly down into its socket. It was the piston of the hydraulic lift that had carried the helicopter up to its exit port.

There was no sound of machinery anywhere. But presently a doubled loop of flexible cable appeared at the ceiling of the cavern. The square platform of the lift followed down. It settled smoothly into view, and then into the pit from which the shaft had risen, filling it completely. The helicopter rested on it, its broad ski landing-gear still choked with snow. There were figures on the lift, some of them in uniform. One of the helicopter's rotor blades was slightly bent.

The flight sergeant stepped off the lift and came over to Sam, as the crew members strained to roll the flying craft off its platform.

"The other heli's back, sir, and wants to come in. So we're sending the lift back up. We got one of the men from the crevasse, sir. Eighty feet down, wedged fast. There's a neat job of a microwave set on him, sir. Smashed, but interesting."

The helicopter was clear of the lift, which rose smoothly and silently toward the square hole in the ceiling overhead. It vanished, but the glistening column rose and rose and rose. The girl's brother climbed down. A stretcher on rollers came forward with two medics pushing it. The helicopter crew lowered a snow-covered, frozen shape. The medics put it on the stretcher.

The girl's brother, Jerry, rubbed his hands and stamped his feet to warm them. She smiled at him. Sam went over to look down at the figure of the man who by possession of a microwave set, by digging into a snowbank to find one of the main transmitters of the Burrow, and who by allegedly shooting at people who met him in the mountains had proved himself a spy trying to locate the Burrow for the enemy.

He looked down at the frozen, now-composed features. He stiffened. He felt the blood drain from his face. But this time no rage, no pain. Only an emptiness.

94

Betty had moved from her brother's side, closer to Sam.

He turned to her.

"You said you found this man on a snow field, and when you shouted to him he shot at you and ran away—to his death. I happen to recognize him, and I think you will. He was one of your closest friends when we were going around together."

He turned and walked away.

8

THE WORLD WAS A VAST GLOBE ROLLING through space. One side was dark, and on that side it was night. The other side was bright, and white clouds floated here and there; waves danced in the sunlight; flowers stood with their pretty vapid faces turned sunward; winds blew and birds dug worms and caroled erotic melodies; fish swam and sheep grazed placidly. On this side all of nature appeared normal.

All but the human race.

In remote small hamlets, to be sure, there was no agitation. The rural villages of Greece and the Balkans were undisturbed. The fellahin of Egypt labored as usual. The blessedly ignorant savages of the Congo were unconcerned and in the Ukraine men contemplated their crops. But in the cities of the world there was panic, now that atomic war was begun.

Naples and Rome and Genoa **were in**describable shambles. Whole quarters of Budapest were ashes. Paris was still a fighting, shrieking madhouse. London police were desperately dynamiting buildings to open new avenues of escape for the hordes of humans trapped by the flames that raged unchecked. All of Holland was in turmoil: its population struggled not only to escape the cities, but the lowlands which would be flooded if the dykes were shattered. Brussels was one monstrous tumult of crazy departure. Moscow was in flight. Atomic war had begun!

The panic was not confined to Europe. From Alexandria and Tunis and Aleppo, streams of fugitives lined the roads, and in the emptying cities behind the refugees skulking figures moved feverishly. The sound of shots and screams was almost commonplace. Rio de Janeiro had become crazed with fear. Buenos Aires—with greater reason, perhaps—was a boiling mass of screaming humanity, fighting to get clear. Singapore was on fire. There the police were hampered by the mass exodus, and the firefighters were helpless against the looters who had set the flames. Capetown was in process of evacuation. Adelaide and Sydney streamed with fleeing folk. All over the world, on every continent, humanity fled the skies.

Railroad trains steamed slowly through France, so incredibly crowded that the toppling of figures from the roofs of cars was no longer heeded by anyone. In Germany the city folk were less numerous, because their ruined cities were not yet rebuilt, but they were most terrified of all—perhaps because they suspected themselves. They fled, their faces pinched not only with terror but despair. Everywhere there were murders and robberies and rapings. There were looting and arson and revolt. Creatures of the slums proved again that slums are the most deadly of national vices, and there were chaos and the certainty of the coming of plague.

In eighteen hours after the falling of bombs upon America, there were eight hundred thousand dead in western Europe alone, and the end was not yet. But not one bomb had fallen anywhere but in America. They—and those who died elsewhere—had died of the bare knowledge that there was atomic war.

Nobody knew who was responsible. Death was loose upon the earth. Seventy millions of human beings had been murdered by assailants yet unknown. Because of this, the murderers must continue their work until they were supreme on earth. They would not dare to stop until their murders had made them safe against all the fury of survivors. . . .

But among the tall and austere mountains above Ranier Glacier, the dawn broke in a still tranquillity. Light shone on the mountains and the valleys, and there was such peace and quietude as has always existed in the highlands.

To be sure, on rocky places above the glacier there were fur-clad human figures. They were placed mostly in small slots cut in the living rock. They gave the dawn no attention. Some watched with absorption small dials that were indicators of happenings many miles away and undetectable by human senses. A few years before they would have been of no importance at all. Now they meant more than life or death. They meant the battle maneuverings of unknown murderers whose victory would involve the destruction of everything men had lived by for two thousand years. Furred, tired figures watched small dials and screens on which little dots and indicators moved erratically. They were fighting a holy war. It was more holy .than any other war since the beginning of time, because they fought for everything that distinguished men from beasts.

Down in the control-room of Burrow 89 there were figures grouped about the commander's chair.

Sam reported stiffly that he had recognized the man whose body had been brought from the crevasse. He was one of a considerable group of slightly shady personalities, he said, whom he had found it desirable to avoid—after acquaintance.

"I can name quite a number of them," he said quietly. "If they could be picked up—"

Thale shrugged his shoulders. He did it all the time now, Sam thought dully.

"You knew them in Denver, Sam," he observed, "and there is no Denver any more. The man was a spy, past question. If Denver still stood, a list of his associates might be useful. But either they got away before it was bombed, and your information's useless, or they were there when the bomb fell—and your information's still no good. But there is a chance that the psych men in Personnel might find something in your memories of the bunch that you don't realize is significant. Go talk to them. But you'd better relax a little first. You're too upset now."

He turned to the others in the room. There was a small neat man in tweeds, and a tall man with a military bearing, a swarthy man in ski costume, and a woman with a brittle, sophisticated look. There were a dozen or more in all. There was a young Chinese. There were a Hungarian, a Russian, a Pole.

"Perhaps," Thale told them courteously, "I ought to say something about welcoming you to a place of safety. Unfortunately, I'm afraid that would not be true. It happens that this is the only Burrow of which we are sure the enemy knows the location. Therefore, it is the only one that can afford to expose itself by open communication abroad. We can offer you direct communication with your governments. If any of you happens to know of codes by which your governments can give us information it would be unwise to send in the clear, we will be glad to have you use them. Frankly, though, we will have to know those codes. Also it's entirely possible that one of you represents the government which has attacked us. You will have to be restricted in your movements about the Burrow. Finally, I admit to you that this Burrow and all of us in it may be destroyed on thirty seconds' notice or none at all."

A murmuring sounded in the control-room. It was essentially agreement—not relief, but acceptance. But the tall, military man moved a pace forward. He said cordially, "Congratulations, Major Thale! I am General Warsaw, and I understand you've done remarkably well—knocking down a bomb or two and so on. Most fortunate! I'm most happy to hear it and to have you here. You will be invaluable. Obviously, since I rank you, I shall take command, but I am sure we will get along splendidly!"

"I am afraid, sir," said Thale, "that you do not take command. By the regulations of the Atomic Service, the commanding officer of a Burrow cannot be given orders during time of war. He can only be advised. I will gladly make use of your advice, sir, but I will not accept an order to turn over command of the Burrow."

General Warsaw's features expressed sheer amazement.

"But my dear Major Thale—"

The small man in tweeds said tactfully, "I'd be

very happy, Major Thale, to be put in communication with Downing Street at the earliest possible moment. In the clear, of course."

The man in ski costume smiled, showing even white teeth. He added a second graceful interruption: "And the Quai d'Orsay has probably moved its position, but could I communicate with my government also, Major Thale?"

General Warsaw said almost humorously, "And I will have to ask to be put in communication with the ranking officer of the Atomic Service, Major Thale!"

"Certainly, sir," said Thale without interest. "I've orderlies waiting to guide all of you to Communications, where you'll have every facility. You understand," he added, turning to the others, "that we may have to seem discourteous in view of the fact that we have to assume that one of you may represent the enemy nation."

Again a murmur of acceptance. Thale pressed a button. The door opened. The group from Sun Valley filed out. Thale noted with amusement that even now the group omitted none of the social amenities that they practiced in ordinary times. The men waited for the two women to precede them; representatives of the various nations bowed politely to each other over who should be next to pass through the doorway.

Sam Burton remained.

"You tell me to relax, Fred!" he protested. "But how can I? On my last leave I suspected that bunch, and didn't report it! I was a fool! If I'd used sense, maybe we'd never have been located—"

"You didn't know the location yourself, Sam," said Thale, "so you couldn't have let it out. Anyhow, we need to have one Burrow in the open. Since we're spotted, we're it."

Sam paced furiously up and down the room.

"If there's a bomb knocked down, Fred," he said in a strained voice, "let me go look at it, will you?"

Thale smiled at him.

"Fella," he said, "there aren't but so many of us Americans left. Those who know they've made mistakes are especially rare, and especially valuable. A man who knows he's made a fool of himself is worth a lot more than one who doesn't realize it's possible."

Sam grunted.

"For which reason," said Thale, "I'd like you to talk to that girl. I'm not certain about her. She ought to be a spy, but she and her gang didn't act like spies when one of them was crippled. There are several things wrong with the idea that she's a spy. If she is, she's remarkable. If she isn't—well—maybe she's more remarkable still."

Sam set his lips.

"If she isn't!"

Thale continued imperturbably.

"She knows we suspect her. She should be especially anxious to offer all sorts of evidence to convince us she isn't—unless she accepts the idea that we'll all be killed any moment. There was an emotional crisis of some sort between the two of you, wasn't there?"

Sam hesitated, then nodded.

"If you ever were in love with her, she'll think you still are. No woman is ever able to believe that a man has got over being in love with her. She'll work on you from that angle—if she's a spy. Hm. . . Talk over your mutual friends. You'll refresh your memory of them and get more data for the psych men to work on. Then go to them and talk. It's asking a lot of you, Sam, but we need any sort of clue that'll start us off. We're groping in the dark now. You were mixed up with a crowd that contained at least one spy. There may have been something dropped by someone, unconsciously, that would mean a lot to a counter-intelligence man."

"I don't think I'll get anywhere talking to her anymore," said Sam sourly. "I think I'm ready to go to psych now. But look here! That General Warsaw—"

"He won't take over," said Thale. "This is no job for a brass-hat regular service man like Warsaw. As far as this Burrow is concerned, it's my job and I'm going to do it, General or no General. I—have personal reasons, too. I'm asking you for help, but nobody's going to take this job away from me!"

Thale's manner was quite natural, but Sam looked at him quickly.

"I—haven't said anything," he said awkwardly, "but you know I'm sorry about—Stella and the kid."

Thale nodded.

"Thanks." He went on without a pause. "The radar gang's been working on your hunch about Antarctica. They've got ideas. Almost any time now you may hear a rocket or two going up. They'll take radars to Antarctica a lot quicker than any bombing plane! I think you had an inspiration, Sam. It's almost certainly where the bombs come from.* It's the only place on earth where a base could be built and bombs stocked and men live and murder seventy million people without anybody else knowing about it."

"I think," said Sam slowly, "that Betty—the girl indirectly suggested it. She said that the Burrows seem to prove that people could keep on living even if a new Ice Age came. And it's true. A deuterium pile gives us heat underneath a glacier. A Burrow'd be quite practical in the Antarctic."

"I suspect," said Thale, "that we're going to find them there. But if we blast them, they'll be obliterated like our cities. Not a trace left. We won't know who built or used them, Sam. That's a problem we've got to solve. It calls for detective work on a new plane. But get going, Sam! I'm going to be busy, too."

Sam went out, leaving Thale at his desk with every appearance of no more than normal intentness directed on his task. But Thale's face had lines in it

* "Nations will try to launch sneak attacks of an utterly new kind. Rockets descending from directly overhead will not reveal what nation launched them. Rockets that come to us from the North Pole might have originated anywhere on earth." *The Atomic Story.* John W. Campbell, Jr.

that hadn't been there twenty-four hours earlier. And when he did not know he was being looked at, his eyes sometimes acquired once more that early expression of stunned grief.

Sam was not going to talk to Betty Clarke. That was final. He was going directly to the psych men, to tell them everything he could recall about her and every person she'd known. Every word, gesture, mannerism, intonation. All would be written down. All would be transmitted to other Burrows for examination by other psychologists and counter-intelligence men. There must have been some slip made by somebody which could be uncovered if looked for closely enough, to tell what nation they spied for. Even that, though, would not be actual proof that their nation had murdered America.

He winced inwardly. It was ironic to be beginning a task which should take hours, when the enemy knew where this Burrow was. There should be a new flight of bombs on the way here now. The enemy had wiped out two hundred cities in forty minutes. They had sent a total of only three bombs at this target, the only one which had offered resistance. They should overwhelm it immediately, to destroy the encouragement its survival gave to the others.

Yet, if he were honest with himself, this was not the reason that he flinched as he drew back his hand to rap on the door of Personnel. He was ashamed of it, but what he dreaded most was the necessity to reveal his own shame—and his love for Betty. Even now.

Angrily, he knocked hard on the door and went in without waiting for a reply.

Tenseness pervaded the entire Burrow. While bombs flashed out of emptiness and Burrows vanished one by one, a certain fatalism was possible. If a bomb did not turn up, there was no need to worry. If one did turn up, there would be no time to worry. But Burrow 89 had defeated two attacks, one by a single bomb and one by a pair. Another attack would undoubtedly come in time. It would be—it must be—vastly different in kind and deadliness. And there were now the Perseid meteors to complicate the problem. Fatalism was possible while defense seemed impossible, but worry began when hope was no longer absurd.

Detector-device technicians labored frantically and achieved the impossible. They linked radars and infra-red detectors and computing devices into a complex with very much the discrimination of the human mind, but a much greater speed of reaction. Every man also constituted himself a counter-intelligence expert and sweated at conjuring up devices that could overwhelm the Burrow's defenses, and then defenses which those devices could not overwhelm. Some prospects so envisioned were absurd, but some were grim.

There was always the possibility of attack by a flight of bombs so numerous that some one must get through. There was simply nothing which could be done about that. A flight of twenty atom bombs, or even ten, arriving at half-second intervals, would infallibly leave a monstrous smoking crater where Burrow 89 now lay beneath a glacier's ice. But it was unlikely for one excellent reason. There were at least one hundred and possibly two hundred Burrows to be knocked out. Ten to twenty atomic missiles allotted to each would require a store of bombs sufficient to reduce the rest of the world to chaos. It would require the use of enough bombs to conquer all the rest of the world twice over, and quite possibly the use of most of the bombs accumulated for that purpose. No more than three hundred bombs had smashed the United States. It was unlikely in the extreme that the enemy was prepared to use one thousand to four thousand more to complete America's destruction. The need could not have been anticipated. So the odds were that no such attempt would be made until all more economical means had failed.

The enemy, in fact, by all the rules of logic should concentrate upon Burrow 89 and use it as a guinea-pig for the development of some new tactic of murder which would destroy it. All other Burrows were necessarily as well prepared as Eighty-Nine to fight off destruction. The time-lag between the failure of one bomb and the possible arrival of the next enabled Eighty-Nine to pass on in detail every feature of its defense. But an attack which wiped out Eighty-Nine could not be described so that other defenses against it could be contrived. Smash Eighty-Nine and the same trick would smash the rest. The psychological effect would help. But Eighty-Nine had to be smashed.

So men sweated to anticipate every possible angle the enemy might develop. There were the Perseids—meteors to be expected every August ninth to twelfth, ranging in size from pinheads to hat boxes and two-family houses. On the dark side of earth they darted here and there against a star-studded sky and looked like pretty fireworks, trailing granular tails of light to be admired. The display was not unusually heavy. On any normal night an average of three shooting stars an hour is visible in any quarter of the sky. The Perseids raised the average to ten or twelve or twenty. That was all. On the day side of earth—and the sun shone on Ranier Glacier—they were not visible. They appeared there only as tiny moving dots in the radar-screens of the Army and of Burrow 89, and corresponding specks on Johnson detectors and infra-red scanners, and in the violently jumping dials of computing machines.

Their speed was from seven miles per second up. The speed of bombs, as previously recorded, had been no more than four. The bombs came from due north—from the North Pole. Until now no moving object in the sky (and there had been plenty of them before the Perseids) had been dangerous save with a speed of four miles per second and a course due south.

But Sam Burton had pointed to Antarctica as an almost certain site for the enemy base. Antarctica is practically the size of Australia, without a single settlement or inhabitant on its shores, and so of course no detection devices unless the enemy used them. To detect bomb-launching sites on Antarctica from Burrow 89 required trickery. Automatic radars could be landed on the southern continent by rockets, but rockets could be detected by their speeds and course. . . .

A trick was devised. Six times during the morning, bombs went up out of the Burrow's launching-tubes. They vanished in the morning sky. And even as they roared away, men worked at a defense against their own trick if the enemy should think of it. And of course the other Burrows were told in top-secret code of the trick and of the defense against it.

The sixth rocket was on its way when Burrow 74, on Catalina Island, triumphantly flashed to all the rest that its detectors had picked up an object checking with the Army radar report by synchronous broadcast of something traveling seven miles a second, moving west to east, and which should have been a Perseid meteor. But the Johnson detector reported that its temperature was wrong. It had not the interstellar chill of the Perseids, which came from far beyond Pluto. An infra-red scanner verified this scandalous news. Snapper-bombs went up to intercept it. One was equipped with a television transmitter and ultra-high-speed scanner. It would not explode against the intruder, but it would transmit to Burrow 74, under Catalina Bay, electrical impulses that could be amplified and converted into light, and fed into an ultra-high-speed camera to produce a strip of film showing all that took place.

Seventy-Four transmitted the film to its companions, and men in every Burrow could look at a squat, ungainly object with a snout-like nose, which masqueraded as a Perseid on its way eastward to dive upon a certain glacier and the folk beneath it. They could see the chemical explosion of the snapper-bombs, infinitely slowed down by the slowing of the film. They could see the beginning of the atomic explosion which took place fifty miles up over the ghastly chasm that had replaced Los Angeles.

Sam Burton saw the film projection run off. Thale called him from his psychological examination to look. He watched in bitter silence as on the film the enemy bomb was detonated.

"The design of that gadget has a flavor," said Thale in an oddly soft voice. "I think I get it. In a sense it's a perfectly standard design, but the feel of it is wrong. It's like a foreigner trying to tell a dialect story in English. No matter how well he speaks English, it never quite comes off. The same thing happens in machines. You can always tell English machinery from French, and French from Russian, and so on. I could make a guess that I'd believe implicitly, of where that rocket was designed. It's evidence, but not proof yet. We don't mention this to our guests."

"No," said Sam.

"We want to be completely sure. . . . You know how a Navy man can tell the nationality of a ship by the way it looks, whether he's seen that design before or not." His voice was suddenly very soft. "I think I know who killed Stella and the kid, now. But I only think so. Before long, maybe, I'll be sure." Irrelevantly, he added, "Our bombs were spotted going to Antarctica by the radar-planes of one of the countries that's helping us. They thought they were Perseids, but they reported them."

Then he stood up.

"Come up to Control, Sam. There's something there I want to show you."

Sam followed, still writhing inwardly at what he had gone through in the psychological room, and further shaken by the picture of the enemy bomb.

"It came from the Pacific," he said abruptly. "It could have come from Antarctica."

"That's right," said Thale with the new strange softness in his voice. "I'm glad of that picture, Sam. It told plenty!"

"Eh?"

"You know how we set off our bombs," said Thale.* "Something very special in the way of a detonator is called for when a bomb hits at four miles a second. But we've got it. I didn't understand why the enemy bombs went off from mere snapper-bomb explosions. I'd hoped to smash one so it wouldn't. But that picture shows that they don't go off from snapper-bomb explosions. They go off because the snapper-bombs are close. They use a proximity-fuse, Sam, so that by no possibility can one of their bombs be brought down intact. They'd rather have 'em explode harmlessly than be brought down whole. They go off if a snapper gets close enough. They're bound to go off if they hit the earth. It's beautiful, Sam! It's beautiful!"

* For a complete discussion of methods of detonating atomic explosives, see "Atomic Energy for Military Purposes," Henry D. Smyth, pp. 211, 212, ref. 12.16 and 12.19. The Smyth report is, of course, the official U. S. Government text on atomic bombs.

He laughed. His eyes were very bright.

"Not so clever, those people," he said. "They're smart in electronics. They control their rockets electronically, Sam. But we were the people who worked out the tricks they've used to murder us! They're not clever to use our own stuff against us, Sam! Not clever at all!"

They reached the control-room. A non-commissioned officer stood up and saluted. He looked stubborn and angry. Major-General Warsaw stalked furiously about the room.

"Major Thale, sir," said the sergeant, "General Warsaw, sir, insisted that I accept his orders. He threatened me with court-martial for insubordination, sir."

"And you obeyed my orders to take none from anyone but myself. Quite right, Sergeant," said Thale. "You will not be court-martialed. You're relieved."

General Warsaw stood in annoyed dignity as the sergeant saluted and went out, his lips moving angrily.

"Your sergeant," he said, in the tone of one trying to be amusedly patient, but not quite succeeding, "is an ass, Major. I would not squabble before an en-

listed man, but he is a fool! I simply asked him to
explain some of the controls. And he acted as if he
thought I was a spy!"

"We're very cagey, sir," said Thale, unsmiling. "A
spy who learns facts about the other Services may do
damage in time of war, but a spy who learns facts
about the Burrows may cause the destruction of an
entire defense-system."

General Warsaw grinned. It was a likeable grin,
Sam thought; perhaps the man was human, after all.

"The deadly secret information I asked was simply which of the controls fires the rockets! I understand they are fired from the control-room."

Thale replied shortly, "The sergeant was not
authorized to tell you, sir. He was quite right to re-
fuse."

General Warsaw made a good-natured gesture of
hopelessness.

"Oh, the devil! My dear Major, I've sent a message to Colonel Graves, of your Service. Was it transmitted to him?"

Thale nodded.

"Then I am fairly sure," said the General, "that
you'll shortly hear from him, instructing you to place
yourself under my orders. Under such circumstances,

is it quite necessary for you to be—you will pardon me, Major—quite so stuffy?"

Thale answered tonelessly, "It's an unpleasant necessity, General; and to avoid further necessities, I'm going to ask you to go to your quarters. Lieutenant Burton will see you there and put a sentry before your door so you won't be disturbed."

General Warsaw's face went blank. His manner, Sam realized now, had been the familiar one of a general who makes a point of being popular with his subordinates. For he now showed just such a general's apoplectic rage on discovering his condescension unappreciated.

"You—wha-a-a-t?" he roared. "What the devil do you mean by that, sir?"

"I'm busy," said Thale bluntly. "This is a highly technical Service, and the niceties of military courtesy take up time. I can't waste it. Especially since I've heard from Colonel Graves and he's coming here and he may—you tell me—relieve me of duty. I've work to do before that happens. See the General to his quarters and arrange about the sentry, Sam."

He sat down at his desk and pushed communicator buttons. Sam moved suggestively. General Warsaw, with tightly-compressed lips, stalked from the control-room. Sam followed. He trailed the General at a discreet distance as he marched down the corridors, trembling with outraged dignity. Then Sam beckoned to the non-com in charge of the guard outside the Math Room—placed there since the arrival of the party from Sun Valley. He gave orders and returned to the control-room as Thale completed instructions over a communicator.

"—Transmit the drawings to other Burrows," said Thale into the transmitter, "with the reasons I just gave you. And hurry up as many samples as can be turned out. It's urgent!"

He turned to greet Sam again.

"There's going to be a shortage of spot-welders in the machine-shop," he said with something close to a grin. "We're going to rob them of parts to fight bombs with. But I wanted to show you the stuff we got off the dead man. He had a notebook, and I asked Graves to come and look at it, because he's made a hobby of handwriting, but what I want to show you is the microwave set he had on him. You know what we both think about the outline of the enemy bomb. This set was made in the United States. There's no question about it. But—"

He pointed. The small radio transmitter had been opened for examination.

"An American wouldn't design a set that way," he went on. "Consciously or not, all American technical designs are conditioned by the processes of assembly-line manufacture. Whether we realize it or not, the way we put things together works out to more or less good assembly-line practice. But a foreigner designed this set and had it turned out in an American plant. They couldn't change details, or it wouldn't work. So—look at it. We could find the plant and track back the customer if there hadn't been a bombing, but it's a blind alley."

Sam's lips set. Everything was a blind alley. The cities, where all clues to enemy espionage must have been located, were no longer in existence. Clues were not clues, for they led only to bomb-craters where cities had been. Still—

"I've seen a set put together like this," said Sam suddenly. "Not a microwave, but the leads were ganged together in just this fashion. It's rather distinctive. The man who had it had bought it abroad. In—"

He stopped, instinctively.

"Yes," said Thale, nodding. "It checks. Funny,

eh? We're like detectives who've found evidence which really pins a crime on somebody, but won't actually convict him. It's only circumstantial evidence. We can't risk acting on it. If it were wrong, we'd be doing murder to our murderers' specifications."

"But there's no way to get proof!" protested Sam.

"We've got to work out a way," said Thale. "I'm working on it. . . ."

"If you're thinking again of using that girl to get proof," said Sam, "you'd better take me off the job. I'm no good at it."

Thale looked thoughtful.

"I talked to Graves about her, and he wants her treated as if we'd changed our minds about suspecting her. Nothing official, you understand. Just relaxing guard, and so on. So your current orders are to treat her as if she's been completely cleared of all suspicion. Only you can't officially tell her so yet."

Sam jumped up.

"Current orders! I didn't take your suggestion as orders before, Fred. I didn't go back to her; I went right to psych. And God knows that was bad enough!"

He stopped for a moment. Then he began talking again, fast.

"Listen. There were a few people murdered yesterday. Some seventy-odd million, in fact. And that microwave set is fair evidence of who did it. This Burrow was made and we were sent to man it, to get even if anything like that happened. Can't you think of anything more useful for me to do than trying to play pattycake with a girl?"

Thale smiled faintly.

"Not at the moment. There won't be much to do until we knock down a bomb. Right now we're detectives, waiting for a laboratory report on evidence we still have to gather. I rather think there's a clue or two on the way, though. At four miles a second." Then he added gently, "I'm not just fiddling, Sam, when a whole world is burning. No, those are orders."

Sam stalked out.

The Burrow went about its business—which made it seem strangely empty. The recreation rooms had no one in them at all. The cavern courts were a blaze of lights, but nobody played tennis or badminton. The shops in which the Wacs spent most of their time and all their pay were deserted. Sam

123

walked down emptily echoing corridors, while the rest of the garrison of Burrow 89 was at the surface, making ready defenses against bombs which might —might!—be handled in ones or twos, but quite certainly couldn't be fought off in numbers.

He was lonely. That was the only way he could describe it—lonely and miserable. The grief at their common losses drew the others together in a companionship he could not now share. Up to now he had shared it, without realizing it. For up to now, although he had had no family to lose, he had been, as a part of the Service, a part of a very intimate and significant family. Without questioning his faith, he had been a part of them by sharing that faith with them—a belief that the things they had lived for were worth dying for.

Then, suddenly, he had realized, with the apparently complete success of the bombing, that he had accepted a comfortable belief by contagion. One had to pay for faith, and he'd had no price to pay. It was not that he was not willing. But the way in which his whole subconscious self had risen to make a woman more important to him than everything else now alienated him from the rest, who had suffered losses without a whimper. There was only one way to atone. That was what he was doing: making an errand of atonement. . . .

Betty Clarke sat listening quietly to one of the women from Sun Valley, who had apparently just discovered that diplomatic immunity was not recognized in atomic war. She was the smartly groomed wife of a foreign attaché, but at the moment she was practically hysterical. In normal times, words that ran counter to her desires were merely displeasing sounds without meaning. But now she had somehow come to realize that the wholesale slaughter of which she had heard was not merely news of diplomatic importance, but a fact she was likely to experience. Unable to reach anyone in authority, she demanded shrilly of Betty Clarke that someone take her immediately to a place of safety.

Betty rose and came quickly when she saw Sam. She led him away from the diplomat's wife.

"I'm doing you a favor, Sam, in steering you away," she said with her odd little one-sided smile. "Revolting as I may be, a scared spoiled woman is worse. Is there news you can tell me?"

He shook his head. There was news, but it was not to be told. It wasn't certainty yet. He and Thale felt

125

that they knew who had bombed America, but the ganging of wires in a microwave set was not evidence on which to destroy a nation. There must be more. Much more. The bombs must be traced back to their launching-tubes, and back beyond that to those who handled them, and beyond that to those who had ordered them fired upon an unsuspecting continent. It was probable that they came from Antarctica. Presently that would be sure. When it was, the Antarctic launching sites would be destroyed. But even then the murder of the United States could not be avenged until the identity of the ultimate criminals was known past any possibility of error.

"We've found out some things," he told her. "We've got some evidence. Even if this Burrow is knocked out, I believe that those who have murdered America will pay for it. But that won't be enough."

Somehow it was easier than he had expected to carry out his orders to treat her as if she were no longer suspected. Somehow it didn't even seem deception any longer. There could be no reason except fatigue; he must simply by now be drained of a capacity for emotion.

She shook her head, lost in thought.

"We probably won't do the destroying ourselves—

this Burrow, that is," he admitted. "We can be knocked out any time, simply by having so many bombs come at us that we can't handle them. But the people who bombed America will lose out. They have to, for things to make sense. Since atom bombs exist, it has to become certain that no people will ever again trust themselves to criminal fools of leaders with notions of conquest. Somehow, atom bombs make it necessary that no country shall ever dare to sell itself to politicians for promises of glory. We Americans have counted heavily on ideals in international affairs. They haven't worked. The living terror of sudden death has to be put into every man on earth, so that he'll be in deadly terror of ever ceasing to be a free man, or of his country's ever ceasing to be a free land. All that simply has to come! And what's happened to America will be pretty mild compared to what will have to happen to somebody else, to make freedom plainly the only way to live."

She said abruptly, "And you're sure you know who sent the bombs?"

"Not yet. But we will be. Somehow."

She looked at him tentatively.

"Do you still believe—"

She stopped. Now was the time, and he suddenly

found the words hard—hard to choose and hard to say. He must not change too suddenly, yet he must give her a feeling of confidence.

"I—don't know," he said. "Perhaps I jumped to conclusions. Thale seems to think you innocent. I'm reserving my opinion. But I'm giving you the benefit of the doubt. To prove it—how would you like to go up to the surface with me? I'd like to see the sun again."

Her voice belied the enthusiasm of her words; it was quiet, restrained.

"I'd love to."

He led the way. It was a tiny lift, and it rose straight up for fifteen hundred feet. They stood in it silently, a little awkwardly. When they reached the top they were in a small, slotted opening roofed and camouflaged into the mountaintop. No climber would ever reach here by accident, but the Burrow had given up all concealment, anyway. Men worked at something which looked like a gun-emplacement, save that no weapon appeared.

They stood in the open, looking out across illimitable distances. Mountains and snowfields and valleys with green areas at their hearts stretched away and away until the eye grew weary of looking at them. But very far off indeed, at the very limit of vision, there was greenness which went on beyond the edge of the world. In between there was sunshine, and snow-white clouds were floating peacefully beneath a sky of translucent blue.

They looked. There was no railing nor any guard. Sam took the girl's hand as a safeguard, and kept it because he wanted to. Even now, it was true: he wanted to. And he didn't know how to begin his task.

The laboring men were lowering a squat smooth object into a hollow in the rock. Sam looked at it and shook his head.

"What's that?"

"New gadget, sir," said one of the men. "Major Thale dreamed it up. All the Burrows are building 'em to try. A fella in Radar said that this trick oughta finish up the job."

10

BURROW FORTY-THREE, IN THE SIERRAS, spotted the second bomb to masquerade as a Perseid. It was sixty miles high, and it traveled northeast, slanting downward; its speed was five miles per second. The Johnson detectors and the infra-red scanners revealed it instantly as an impostor. Ravening things went roaring up to meet it. Among them were two specimens of a new device. They had been snapper-bombs, but they were modified. The thousand-pound charges of chemical explosive had been removed, and their noses were spun-metal hoods of a new form. There were within them innocuous-seeming, close-packed rolls of tin foil robbed from electric spot-welding devices in the Burrow's machine shop. They contained also an extraordinarily sturdy oscillator tube apiece, made to handle a kilowatt of current. There was nothing deadly in them. Nothing. But their mass was less than that of a normal snapper-bomb, and their fuel stores and drive-tubes were unchanged. The unmodified snapper-bombs sent up with them were left behind. Their acceleration was four thousand six hundred feet per second.

The twin devices flashed upward almost level with each other. At thirty miles their drives went off. At forty they went on again in momentary, furious flashes. At fifty they spouted flame in jets too brief to be separated by the eye. They reached the altitude and surpassed the speed of the rocket which masqueraded as a meteor. In identical, infinitely graceful arcs they converged upon it.

And that was all. Nothing seemed to happen. They went on past. But many, many miles below, the operator of a Johnson detector made a sober-voiced report and then arose from his instrument and danced. And raging snapper-bombs came roaring upon the bomb—still slanting toward the earth at almost sixty miles up. Their chemical explosives flared brightly against the dark purple sky, and still nothing happened. And detection-device operators observed the total absence of any atomic flame in the upper stratosphere, and threw back their heads and howled with glee.

The news flickered from Burrow to Burrow in the most closely guarded of top-secret codes. But Burrow 89 knew before the news could be put in code, and long before it could be transmitted and received and decoded again. The radars said that the object was coming in over the Sierras at five miles per second, slanting very slowly and gradually downward. The infra-red scanners said its temperature had risen four degrees, very suddenly. Two more of the new devices went up, leaving behind their snapper-bomb companions.

But they did not even curve toward the enemy object. They went on up, straight up, and when their drives cut off they stayed off. They ignored the enemy bomb. They went on out and out as if the bomb had not been there. And the slower but still lightning-like snapper-bombs came and exploded all about it, and there was no difference at all. . . .

The bomb went on. It passed six miles overhead and four miles to the northwestward of Burrow

89, and it struck on the reverse slope of Mount Man-ifred—seventy miles away—and it gouged a deep furrow, and bounced out of the earth, and set fire to a small pine-forest and rocketed insanely down the length of a minor valley and came to rest barely underground. It had not exploded.

Back in the Burrow—his errand an abject failure, but a new plan buzzing in his head—Sam Burton watched blankly as Thale plucked small objects from the drawers of the commander's desk and stuffed them in his pockets. Thale's eyes were very bright. The tension was gone from his face. Even the grayish pallor of his skin had lessened. He smiled at Sam as he picked up a small tooled leather picture-frame from the desk-top and took out the picture of a six-year-old, tucking it carefully into an inside pocket.

"What's all this?" demanded Sam.

"The war's about over for me," said Thale.

Sam swore angrily.

"You mean Colonel Graves—"

"I've talked to him," Thale replied. "He's writ-ten a report for me on that spy's notebook. And he agrees with what I'm going to do. It's the only pos-sible thing, Sam, and I'm the only possible person."

"The devil!" protested Sam furiously. "He hasn't turned over command of this Burrow to that fatuous ass Warsaw, has he? Dammit, Fred, I came to see you about something important! That third chap we picked up on the glacier—the one with the wrenched tendon—has done a lot of traveling. He tells me he's always had a wretched time with his teeth. He's visited dentists in every country abroad, and he says their work's inferior. They're not up to American dentists technically and besides, their gold fillings don't stand up."

Thale stared, and then whistled softly.

"Good!" said Thale. "Beautiful! We should have thought of that before! Can you attend to it, Sam? It's a bit odd, but the fellows who get out the plutonium from the pile down below should be able to run a microanalysis* for you."

* For the quality of chemical research during the development of the atomic bomb, see "Atomic Energy for Military Purposes," Henry D. Smyth. For example, p. 101, ref. 6.34.*** "one microgram is considered sufficient to carry out weighing experiments, titrations, solubility studies, etc." Three five-gram aspirin tablets weigh a little over one gram. A microgram is one one-millionth part of the weight of three aspirin tablets. The thousandth part of a thousandth part.

"I can take care of it," protested Sam. "But dammit—"

The door of the control-room opened. Major-General Warsaw, triumphantly military and vindictive in a general-officer fashion, came in with Colonel Graves, who had arrived at Burrow 89 an hour previously. At the sight of Thale, his expression grew stern. Colonel Graves, however, looked amused.

"Thale, consider that you've had a reprimand for having put General Warsaw under arrest," he said.

Thale replied stiffly, "Yes, sir."

"He tells me," Graves went on, "that he asked a perfectly innocent question of the sergeant on duty in the control-room, here, and that the sergeant not only refused to answer, but acted in a definitely disrespectful manner. Moreover, he tells me that you told the sergeant he was quite right in refusing."

"Yes, sir," said Thale. "He was."

General Warsaw did not look pleased, but he broke in a little condescendingly.

"The reprimand having been given, my dear Colonel, suppose we call the matter settled. After all, Major Thale is a junior officer and this is his first command. He is entitled to a certain excess of zeal, and to communicate it to his subordinates. If he is prepared to call the matter quits, and to understand that next time it would be a much more serious matter, I am sure we shall be able to get along excellently in the future."

He looked at Thale in the manner of a general officer who has most generously waived his just resentment, and expects his generosity to be appreciated. Thale, however, gave no sign. But Sam Burton's hands clenched, and he drew in his breath sharply.

"Now to clean up the other matters," Colonel Graves went on smoothly. "I looked over the notebook taken from the dead spy. Every word in it is in English and on its surface it's merely the normal notebook of a man with a partiality for—I gathered —blondes. Still, there are points in it. I've written a memorandum concerning it."

"Yes, sir," said Thale woodenly.

"Now," said Graves briskly, "there's one more item. We couldn't handle the notebook matter over a vision circuit and it was quite worth my coming here to look at. But I've got to be getting back to my own post, in case of action. So let's be quick about the rest. I believe you picked up three

136

people on the glacier overhead, one of whom led you to that spy's body?"

"Yes, sir," said Thale. "Sam, will you have the young lady brought here?"

Sam picked up a communicator and spoke into it. His voice was quiet, but he was raging. General Warsaw had beamed at Thale. It was the condescending, triumphant, kindly beam of the most offensive of all types of general officer—the sort who fancies himself the idol of his men. But since Thale had neither fawned nor groveled after authoritative intercession in his behalf, General Warsaw had gradually begun to grow indignant. Every sign now pointed to his intention to rank Thale out of his command and to the intention of Graves—senior in the Atomic Service—to permit him to do so. Sam felt like mutiny.

There was a tap on the door. An orderly escorted Betty Clarke into the room, saluted smartly, and departed. She looked about her, saw Sam and Thale, saw General Warsaw and paled a little, and saw Colonel Graves. She seemed more nervous than Sam had ever seen her. Her fingers fumbled with her handkerchief. Automatically they rolled it and tied it in that curiously complicated knot that looked like a rosette.

There was an odd, sustained silence in the control-room. Betty Clarke nervously pulled at the ends of the handkerchief, and the knot came out again. She tied it a second time, looking from one to the other of them. And still the silence persisted. Sam, staring stupidly at her, observed with a kind of drugged interest that the new knot was different.

"Er—Miss Clarke," said Colonel Graves. "I understand—"

General Warsaw held up his hand.

"One moment, my dear Colonel!" he said, in what was definitely the voice of a general officer taking control of a situation. "One moment! I think I know this young woman! I have barely met her—once only, I believe—but I have wished most earnestly to meet her again! She was the cause of a most unfortunate incident, by which a very promising young officer was led into an indiscretion that ruined his military career!"

Betty glanced furtively at Sam. He closed his eyes. On top of all the rest—

"There was little evidence," said General Warsaw sternly, "but the indications pointed strongly

—very strongly, I may say—to the conclusion that the young lady was the agent of a foreign power. To find her here is the strongest possible reason to suspect that military information has passed or will pass—possibly even that the apparent success of this Burrow in detonating enemy bombs is not all that it seems to be."

Colonel Graves moved forward.

"You mean she's definitely a spy?" he asked mildly.

"You will find the records of the case, with all the data from which conclusions should be drawn, in—"

Colonel Graves smiled broadly. His fist shot out with the speed and suddenness of a striking snake. There was a distinct loud crack. General Warsaw hurtled backward. He hit the floor with a crash.

"I didn't want to give him a chance to pull a gun," said Colonel Graves apologetically, "and of course I wanted someone else at hand. The man was damned good! I wonder who he is!"

He blew on his knuckles and looked up at Thale and at Sam, who was staring at him incredulously.

"Miss Betty Clarke," he said dryly, "is counter-espionage. I've known her all her life, and she's been reporting to me for years—at least ever since she's been old enough to meddle in such matters. I've had no report from her for nearly a week, but things have been moving rather fast."

Betty Clarke said quickly, "Do you remember, Colonel, that I—once reported on a—Lieutenant Burton who it was feared might be indiscreet? And —that I said he—was all right?"

"Eh?" Then Colonel Graves glanced at Sam. "Oh! . . . Oh, yes! To be sure!" Then he bent over and rolled back the eyelids of the unconscious man on the floor. "What'll you do with this chap? I've no idea who he is, except that he certainly isn't General Warsaw. He'd have known that little recognition-knot you tied, Betty, if he had been. And he'd have seen when you tied the second knot that said there was a spy in the room."

"He was a spy—I met him once," said Betty. Her voice shook a little. She very carefully did not look at Sam. "He knew the men whom Steve and Jerry and I had traced up into the mountains. The ones we came after. The ones who fell into a crevasse. . . ."

"And who were specifically spies," said Graves. "Hm . . . Not much doubt of him, then. I imagine he denounced you because you'd met him in civilian clothes, using another name. He hoped to rank someone out of command of a Burrow, I suppose, and fire a few bombs that would set all Europe to fighting. But what will you do with him?"

Sam Burton moved forward. In spite of himself, he was grinning.

"I suggest that we pry a gold filling out of one of his teeth, for one thing."

"An inspiration!" said Thale, smiling with bright eyes. He put his hand on Sam's shoulder. "I'm going off as you know, Colonel. Sam here is next in rank. He'll take over, unless—"

"The devil!" protested Graves. "I've a sweet-running Burrow of my own! And I mean to be back there punching the firing-buttons when the time comes. May it be soon!"

"It should be," said Thale softly. "We've had six automatic radars in Antarctica for four hours. They gave us fixes when the bomb that just crash-landed took off. We've got four more on the way south now, to fine down the fix a bit. When I set to work up here, they'll throw everything they've got at me, and we ought to have the locations to perfection. Eh?"

"We should!" agreed Colonel Graves. "And I've

got to get back to be ready for the happy day. But this fellow—"

Thale pressed a button. He gave orders. Men came in to remove "General Warsaw."

"Lieutenant Burton's taking over command," said Thale quietly. "I'm going to look at the bomb that was knocked down. What orders about the prisoner, Sam?"

"Strip him," said Sam curtly. "Have him watched constantly against suicide, and if he's got a gold or silver filling in a tooth, pull the tooth and turn it over to Medical. I'll instruct them."

He waited until the erstwhile major-general had been carried out. Then he said angrily, "Fred! I asked for that job! I asked for the job of examining any enemy bomb—"

"And you don't get it, Sam," said Thale gently. "It's mine. I want it and I'll take it. The numbness is wearing off. I—" He stopped.

"You're crazy!" protested Sam. "You're crazy, man! You're valuable—"

Thale grinned at him and went out, with Graves. And Sam would have followed them, protesting, but the control-room must never be left empty, however remote from formality the operations of the Atomic Service might be. Sam could not leave. The door closed.

In the utter stillness, Betty stirred. Sam turned. He looked at her for a lone minute.

"Betty—I'm a fool."

Then she was in his arms, and her control finally broke.

"You're not," she said indignantly, and stopped crying long enough to laugh at her own indignation. "Only—it was so hard. When I—came here, I made the recognition—signal to Major Thale, and he saw it but he—didn't make any sign until he'd checked with Colonel Graves. That was right, but I was so afraid he hadn't got it. And—I couldn't tell you, even when— And all the time we might all have been blown to bits, without you ever knowing—"

There was a change on the wall-bank of colored lights which told of the operation of every bit of machinery in the Burrow. The light-change indicated that the helicopter-lift was in operation. A little later it showed that the exit-port was raised. Presently the light-board showed the lift coming down empty. And again it rose. The second helicopter took off. Thale had left his command.

"Thale's gone." said Sam. "He'll never be back.

I'm in command of the Burrow. I thought it would be a great thing, once, to be in command of a Burrow."

"You'll—do all right," said Betty.

A voice spoke abruptly from a speaker close by.

"Reporting, sir, that the prisoner recovered consciousness. And apparently he had some poison that we didn't suspect, sir. There was a bit of adhesive tape— The guard simply saw him keel over dead, sir." There was a pause. *"Further report, sir. He had several gold fillings."*

Sam released Betty.

"Cancel my previous orders," he said. "I'll call Medical."

He did. He also called Communications. He gave orders to Math. He summoned the can-room, far down in the bowels of the earth, and switched in a television screen that he might reassure himself that everything was ready. But those things were needless. Time passed, and time passed, and time passed. Betty stood near him, and he reached out a hand and held hers tightly.

At last he turned on the loud-speaker which was tuned to amateur wave-bands. They were very nearly silent. A voice said thinly: *". . . at last report there was no word of any invasion. My batteries are getting low and I'll have to sign off because there's no power to recharge them. . . ."* On a different wave-band a voice chattered despairingly, *"For God's sake, somebody on the West Coast answer! My girl's in Pasadena! Has it been hit yet?"* And a third voice, *". . . batteries low . . no way to rechar— . . . -ning off. . . ."*

Betty brought a chair from the corner of the room and placed it beside him. After a moment she asked, "A bomb was knocked down and didn't explode. Is that right?"

"It was Thale's work," he told her. "Good work, too. Another Burrow got a film that showed a bomb detonated by our snapper-bombs. It was clear that the enemy's using proximity fuses—a sort of fuse that sends out a radar-signal and picks up its echo and detonates the bomb when the echo makes a certain beat-note that depends on distance. We don't use those fuses on our bombs, for a very good reason. The enemy evidently doesn't know that reason. So he'd probably be using an electronic course-control as well. Thale applied the tactic that we anticipated when we stopped using both tricks."

145

It was very quiet in the control room. In a little while, Sam went on.

"Thale had a couple of snapper-bombs changed. Loaded them up with charged condensers and put in a one-kilowatt radio tube and a beam antenna. He had their radar-control changed so that they didn't send out a signal of their own, but would follow a proximity fuse signal home and when it got strong enough trip a relay. You see the idea?"

She shook her head. She was a listener, a shadowy figure in the semi-dark room with its banks of tiny colored lights and its now-blank row of television screens. Before Sam on the commander's desk was the grim, hooded row of launching-tube firing-buttons.

"A condenser's like a compressed-air tank, after a fashion. You can store electricity in it under pressure. You can get it all out in a fraction of a second, and you can store a lot in it, but you can't let it out again little by little. It has to come out again in a rush. Automatic spot-welders use the trick, storing up electricity from a small current and then letting it all out again in a terrific surge. That's what the new bombs were designed to do. Other Burrows, of course, made them when they got the design and the reason for them. . . ."

He paused. A speaker by his ear had clicked. But it clicked off again.

"Burrow 43 spotted a bomb. They sent up two modified snappers—blow-out bombs. They ran into the radio waves the bomb's fuse was sending out. They swung into line with them. They went for that bomb like homing pigeons. And when they got close—but not close enough to set off the bomb—little relays clicked, and all the electricity in all the condensers poured out like lightning-flashes. It poured through their one-kilowatt radio tubes, which are supposed to burn four thousand hours. It burned them out in the hundredth part of a second. But it made beams of medium radio-waves of two million kilowatts power—for the hundredth part of a second. Four million kilowatts of power in two beams. They actually heated the bomb by four degrees. But they weren't the right wave-length to detonate it. Instead, they burned out every radio-tube in the fuse, and every other tube in the bomb with it. They exploded the filaments in the tubes the enemy used not only to explode his bomb, but to guide it. The bomb couldn't go off. More than

147

that, it couldn't be aimed any more. They control their bombs by radio tubes, but we gave up the idea because we found out better. Their bomb became just a hunk of matter rolling along in the stratosphere."

A voice muttered in his ear. He said quietly into a transmitter, "The fillings in both sets of teeth agree, eh? I thought they would! Thanks!"

He went on steadily, "There's more to it. We'd thought the enemy bombs might be coming from Antarctica. We wanted to send automatic radars there—quicker than planes could take them. We didn't want the enemy to know they were there. So we figured we'd send them by rocket. We mounted them on rockets for the purpose. Then we figured out tricks to make our rockets simulate meteors, so if the enemy radars detected them they wouldn't be suspicious of them. We sent them in on crazy courses at meteor speeds. There's an air patrol across the South Pacific, by the way, and they reported them, but as meteors."

Betty was excited.

"That was clever!"

"Not particularly. It just hadn't been tried before. And then we guessed the enemy might try the same trick, so we got set to catch him at it. And we did. We exploded his first bomb to try it. He was at a disadvantage, you see. His bombs might move like meteors, but they always headed straight for a Burrow. We figured he'd correct that next time, and we had modified snappers with their blow-out beams ready. He did correct it. He sent a bomb drifting along that wasn't aimed at any Burrow. Forty-Three spotted it by its temperature. Johnson detectors and infra-red scanners did the job. The enemy figured we'd detect it and dismiss it as harmless, and at the last minute he'd pile on power, change its course to slam us—and go to town. But he couldn't. We'd spotted it and burned out all its controls. It couldn't put on power or change course. It was dead. And it landed. Thale's gone to look it over."

"And?" she asked softly.

"He's a dead man and he knows it," said Sam. "But he's glad. On account of his wife and kid. I'm waiting for him to come in now on television."

A voice muttered from the loud-speaker. He answered, "Of course!"

A television screen flickered, and abruptly formed a picture. It was of a part of a valley, and

149

there was a monstrous upheaval of dirt, and the drive-tubes of a rocket were visible. Thale moved into view, approaching the rocket with a torch in his hand. His voice came casually from a speaker.

"A throat-mike's a useful invention, Sam. We uncovered this thing and I've sent the work-gang away. Communications will be photographing everything the screen shows, and recording my voice too, I hope. I'm not going to move the lens until I've loosened a couple of plates. I don't think they'll have booby-trapped this part of the gadget. They'd expect us to try to disarm the bomb first. I haven't time."

He labored, only partly visible. Then he could be seen to stoop and stare. He laughed suddenly. Genuinely.

"You'll get a kick out of this, Sam! The first thing I see is an American motor! Made by Westinghouse! Get the picture, Sam? American parts in an enemy bomb! How'll we find out where their bombs come from if they're assembled from American parts? Aren't they clever?"

He bent down and worked again. For moments he said nothing. The speaker gave out only gruntings. Then a chuckle.

"The wiring-cable's American, too, Sam! The guys are getting too smart! They take every precaution against a bomb being examined, but they make it of American stuff regardless, just in case! —Oh, oh! Here's an electronic relay. This you should see!"

The screen showed him approaching. The scene wabbled and shook as he carried the television lens to a new position. There was a new and closer view of the rocket, from which plating had been partly cut away with a thermit torch.

"Get some good pictures of this! Radio tubes by RCA! Sockets by General Electric! They must have chuckled at this when they laid it out! But look at the layout, Sam. The stuff's American, but the way they used it isn't!"

The lens shifted again.

"Get those pipe-joints. Look at this fuel-pump position. The pump's a Delco job, Sam! The position of the fuel-pump's the one we dropped five years ago. Too clever to be practical. This type of gasket is odd. I'm going to focus on one. Get good sharp pictures if you can. . . ."

In the control-room of the Burrow, Betty whispered, "Won't spies pick this up?"

"They will!" said Sam bitterly. "And they'll notify our enemies. They've probably done it already. But they can't get the pictures because we use a tricky scanning-pattern. They won't get the voice, either. We've a trick on that too. But they know what's happening, damn them!"

Thale's voice went on. He wasn't detached, now, or absorbed in something else. Almost gleefully he called the roll of American manufacturers who had made this part or that of the enemy bomb. He worked with smooth haste, dismantling the rocket-drive, the fuel-control, the ignition system.

He was at this point when a voice muttered from a speaker in the control-room.

"We've got the fixes in Antarctica, sir. They check each other. Ten bombs on the way. What'll we do, sir?"

"Calling Math!" snapped Sam. "You have the radar fixes? Courses set?"

A tinny voice replied, *"Right! Tubes Two, Six, Seven, Ten, sir, ready to fire."*

Sam savagely thrust his thumb on a button before him. A roaring whine began deep underfoot. *"Whooo-ooo—OOO-OOO-OOOOMMM!"* It rose and became a trembling noise that shook the very stone. He stabbed a second button. A third and fourth. *"Whooo-ooo-OOOO-OOOOOOMMM!"* *"Whooo-ooo-OOO-OOOO-OOOOOMMM!"* *"Whooo-ooo-OOOOO-OOOOOMMM!"*

Sam swore under his breath as the thunder died away.

"You—fired rockets?" Betty still whispered.

"I did!" raged Sam. "We had ten automatic radars down where the enemy bombs come from. Six spotted the last two bombs as they rose. We sent down four more to make the fix more exact. Ten bombs were just fired—at Thale, I'm pretty sure, because they must know what he's after. Our radars spotted those ten bombs as they went up. We've got the location from which the bombs that smashed America were fired! And all the Burrows shared up the job of smashing them. We sort of drew lots, and the lucky ones fired four bombs apiece, two at each of the bases the enemy's got down there. They're eleven thousand miles away and we've never seen them. And we never will, because, by God, we've sent more atom bombs to blast those two bases than they dropped on all of America! They'll be blown to atoms and those atoms into atoms! A hundred miles around our targets will be one monstrous crater.

There'll be nothing left of them. Less than nothing! But it still isn't enough!"

The figure of his friend Fred Thale moved on the television screen. Fred Thale's voice came out. His expression was joyously intent.

"Communications!" rasped Sam. "Tell Major Thale that bombs are on the way. He's got better than half an hour. We'll send for him! He's done enough!"

He clenched his hands, waiting for the message to get through. After a moment Thale looked up, then he looked at his watch. He grinned from the screen at Sam.

"Too much yet to do, Sam. I won't leave this job. We've got to make it positive, and I think we're doing it. They're too clever when they use American parts, because they don't know how to use them as we would. They've got the words, but they don't know the music. They do their own designing with an accent. If they'd used their own parts the way they used them would seem natural. But they bungled when they used ours. Look at the way this gadget's put together! The man who made this layout had never designed for an assembly-line!

"Sam—look on the book-shelf in my quarters.

There's a red book there on servo-motors. It's not in English. Compare the illustrations with this! The damned fool who designed this signed the job! You know who did it! And this—"

His voice went on. In ten minutes he had exposed the workings of the gyroscopes, made by Sperry. In twenty, the electronic controls of the gyros and servo-motors. The parts were American but there were little tricks of installation and of placing, of the use of one type of resistor instead of another for a particular purpose. . . . In thirty minutes he had the course-setter opened to view, and the television lens had transmitted to the motion-picture cameras of the Burrow the details of the device used by the enemy to guide his bombs. Separate elements of the device had been made by Elgin.

Sam hounded the surface batteries, demanded that all blow-out bombs be more than ready, that snapper-bombs be set to form a cloud of destruction. There were ten bombs on the way to Thale. None must pass over his home Burrow to get to him!

Thale's voice went on calmly. More than half the plating on the top part of the bomb was off, now, and sunlight shone in upon the maze of twisting pipes and tubes and wires within the rocket's massive

155

frame. The atomic explosive had not been touched. That was the part that ordinarily would have been removed first, for safety. Thale had no thought of safety.

His voice went on, composedly, "Only one man in the world would have used die-castings for this gadget! You know him, Sam. And these circuits were laid out by the man I used to tell you jokes on. The old fellow with the bushy beard. . . ."

In the control-room of the Burrow, four hundred feet under solid rock and that beneath a glacier, Sam Burton found himself snarling as dull concussions came from overhead. They were the rocket-driven defense-bombs, with accelerations of a hundred gravities. They went raging up into the sky. Because enemy bombs were on the way.

Not only Eighty-Nine fought valiantly to knock down the enemy missiles. There were ten of them, and many Burrows fought them bitterly. One bomb was detonated over New Mexico. It had come in from the Pacific over Baja California, and then went in a sweeping curve to northward. A second bomb was detonated by Burrow 74 on Catalina Island. And two were knocked dead by blow-out bombs in Oregon, slanting southward. But there were ten.

"Not bad," said Thale's voice with a deep satisfaction. "You've got the proof now, Sam. The photos will show who designed this thing. The style of the men who designed at least four parts is as distinctive as their signatures would be, and they all belong to one nation—the same we'd other reason to suspect. You can prove to the world who's guilty, now. And I feel good, Sam. You see—"

The television screen went blank.

That was all. The atomic explosion that left a chasm deeper than a mountain where Thale had stood, was too violent to affect the television transmitter before it destroyed it. Seconds later the Burrow rocked and trembled to its depths from the monstrous concussion-waves created by six atomic bombs landing upon one target seventy miles away.

But that impact and that concussion was utterly trivial beside a flame that arose on Antarctica only minutes later, although eleven thousand miles away. Down there more than four hundred bombs—more than had fallen on all of America—descended upon two small areas. The enemy had probably built very fine bases in Antarctica. They were doubtless very well defended. But if any conceivable atomic violence produced by man could ever set off a chain-

157

explosion which could destroy the earth, it would have been set off then. Four hundred atomic bombs on two small areas, when six bombs landing on New York had destroyed eight million people. . . .

When it was over there were two monstrous craters in the Southern continent which went down and down toward the earth's very heart—and began slowly to fill up with molten rock.

11

"WHOOOO-OOOO - *OOOOO* - *OOOOO*-
OOOOOOMMM!"

That was the third rocket-bomb to go up out of
the launching-tubes. As its echoes died away, there
was the sound of exultant shouting—thin and muted
—in the corridors of Burrow 89. In the control room
Sam Burton was very pale. His hands shook. But
as the men from Sun Valley filed into the room, he
took a grim hold on himself. They were the consular attachés and minor diplomats who had been
fortunate enough to have been in Sun Valley instead
of at their posts when the bombs fell on America.
They did not look suave or polished or imperturb-

able now. The Englishman mopped his forehead constantly. The Hungarian stumbled over the threshold. The Chinese was paler than any Caucasian. The Greek's eyes burned. The Pole's hands clenched and unclenched. Each man carried a small, thick sheaf of papers and photographs—neatly stapled together—in his hand.

"Whooo-ooo-OOOO-OOOOOMMM!"

The Burrow shuddered as another atomic missile went on its way. When they heard it, it was already climbing for the vacuum beyond the earth's atmosphere. Once launched, there was no recall. It would travel thousands of miles through emptiness, with the sun shining brightly upon it, and presently it would drop down and down—and there would be a flare of annihilated matter reaching to the stratosphere. That flare would contain the atoms and molecules of houses and machines, and of the very stones of streets, and there would be traces of carbon and hydrogen and other elements which an instant before had been parts of living bodies. But they would not be distinguishable from any others.

The silence in the control room was deadly. One man breathed harshly, with a rasping sound in his throat. All of them fixed their eyes on Sam Burton, standing at the commander's desk.

"The bombardment has begun," he said in a brittle voice. "The first bombs will land in fifteen minutes. Every American Burrow is firing upon prearranged targets. We are completely convinced that we have discovered the nation which murdered our countrymen. The commanders of other Burrows, looking at the evidence you have in your hands, are unanimously agreed."

The Englishman said thickly, "Sir, I— agree that the evidence is enough. In—the name of humanity I can only appeal— The bombs that have been sent cannot be recalled. But—"

He choked. Sam Burton spoke quietly in reply.

"What else can we do? If war is a crime, it must be punished. And human beings are certainly responsible for their governments. They submit to them if they do not support them. A man who lets himself be enslaved, so that his leaders may plan war, commits a crime against humanity. Ultimately his crime is murder. Seventy millions of my countrymen have been murdered by men who let themselves be enslaved. If their crime is not punished so that any man who dreams of repeating it will wake in a cold sweat of terror, how many hundreds of millions more will not be murdered?"

His manner was icily calm, but his hands shook so plainly that he rested them upon the desk to hide their trembling. He pressed a button. The television screens which lined one side of the wall flickered into light. Figures appeared in the squares of light, staring anxiously out into the room.

Steve said to those figures, "What we do may be only a form, but when in the course of human events a people must take such action as is necessary today, a due consideration to the opinion of mankind requires that they state their reasons. Our enemy has murdered seventy millions of our countrymen. Some of them were old, but they had committed no crime against our enemy. Some were men and women in the prime of life, with children whom they guarded joyously. They had done no injury to our enemy. And there were young men and women whose lives were hardly begun, and boys playing baseball and climbing trees, and girls playing with their dolls, and very little girls having tea-parties, and there were babies sleeping in utter contentment. They had not harmed, nor did they make any threat against our enemy. But they are dead. Our enemies murdered them."

He took a deep breath. His face was pinched. A bomb went out of a launching-tube. *"Whoooo-oooo-OOOO-OOOOOOMMM!"* Another one. *"Whooo-oooo-OOOO-OOOOOOMMM!"*

"This is not the only crime. The world was at peace. Every nation on earth had renounced war, save on one condition only. In the Brienne Agreement, every nation pledged itself to use the atomic powers made available to it—by America, it may be said, and England and the Dominion of Canada—to destroy any other nation which made atomic war. The nation which began atomic war thereby notified an end of peace, and the beginning of an age of suspicion and wholesale murder which could not end without the whole earth enslaved or else in ashes. This was a second crime."

A bomb went up. *"Whoooo-oooo-OOOO-OOOO-MMM!"*

"We," said Sam steadily, "are the instruments by which war becomes suicide for the nation which wages it. I am sorry that there are people now alive who will presently be killed. But I cannot help it. I would not dare to try to help it. They may feel that the murder of America was not their doing; that their leaders are the criminals. I say only that in allowing themselves to be enslaved they became criminals. If they are allowed to go free they will become criminals again.

"We Americans are not sending bombs merely to kill our enemies. We are sending bombs also to save the lives of the hundreds of millions who will be murdered if men ever dare to become slaves again, or nations dare to be anything but free. I call upon every other nation to fulfill the Brienne Agreement —to destroy the nation which has invited destruction by the crime of murder. I demand the destruction of every city, every hamlet, every cross-road. I demand that the enemy country be turned into a waste of bomb-craters so that for ten thousand years to come any man who thinks of war will look at it and have his blood turn to ice within him!"

"Whooo-oooo-OOOO-OOOOOMMM!" went the bombs up the launching-chamber. *"Whoooo-oooo-OOOO-OOOOOOMMM!"* The figures in the control-room quivered at the sound. The Englishman wiped sweat from his face again. The Frenchman sobbed suddenly. *"Whoooo-ooooo-OOOOO-OOO-OOOMM!"*

"There is no question of the crime," said Sam, wetting his lips. "The question has been of the murderer. We have been faced, not with the task of indicting a nation, but of convicting it. The enemy did not commit its murders from its own territory, but from bases in Antarctica constructed for the purpose over a probable term of years. We have destroyed those bases more terribly than any man-made thing has ever been destroyed before. One cannot extract evidence from a bomb-crater. But we have found proof elsewhere. For one thing, we know that no rulers of a free nation, who by orderly processes could be replaced by men of other views, would dare to begin a plan for the murder in cold blood of a large part of the human race. The rulers of the nation which is our enemy had to be sure that by fraud or violence they could secure themselves against overthrow by their own people. This was essential if this war was to be prepared for."

On the lighted television screens were shown the figures of a king, and premiers, and there was a general officer with his breast bespangled with medals. There was one figure in an Eastern robe. A premier spoke, and the television screen showed the glinting of liquid drops on his forehead.

"Mon Dieu, but you could make a mistake—"

"You will hear the evidence," said Sam grimly. "Better, I will give you a jury. These men are diplomatic representatives of a dozen nations. You know them, and the value of their word. They have in their hands the evidence of the guilt of the nation we consider our enemy."

The television figures stirred. The Englishman mopped his forehead again. There was the horrible, the terrible, the unspeakably ghastly noise of a bomb hurtling skyward to destroy everything within miles of the spot where it struck. *"Whooo-oooo-OOOOO-OOOOOOMMM!"*

"We caught two spies," said Sam quietly. "From them we extracted teeth containing fillings. One had a notebook. He had also a microwave radio set. An officer of the Atomic Service had made a hobby of comparative handwritings. He examined the notebook. Every word in it was English, but the spy had all unconsciously, now and again, formed certain letters as he had been taught to form them in his childhood. Not as American children are taught, but children using a foreign language. It was evidence, but not proof, of his nationality. He had a microwave set containing certain elements of design which are found only in sets manufactured in a certain country. Again evidence, but not proof."

He paused, caught his breath, and plunged on.

"Both spies, though—and their guilt as spies was unquestionable—had fillings in their teeth. The technique of the dentists in every case had been identical. A packing material behind the metal within the cavities—which could not be examined except in an extracted tooth—was identical. The packing material has never been used, save in one country. The metal of the fillings contained a trace of rhodium. It was spectroscopically minute, but it identified the actual mine from which the gold used to fill these two spies' teeth was taken. The country in which that mine exists does not permit the export of gold. Another indication."

He ignored the whoooooooming noise of bombs going up the launching-tubes. He spoke on, steadily.

"We knocked down an atom bomb, unexploded. Major Thale, of this Burrow, went out and disassembled a good part of it. The parts—motors, electronic elements, pumps, and so on—were made in the United States. The designers of the bomb must have found much amusement in using American parts for the bombs which were to destroy America. But they failed to realize that the designers of machinery have individualities of technique which are as distinctive as the brush-strokes of an artist or the cutting of a tailor. We identified the technique—and presented the diplomatic gentlemen in this room with comparison photographs for examination—of at least four specific men in four specialized assemblies of the bomb we examined. All were of the same nationality. We required only one more proof. We found two."

Bombs went up the launching-tubes.

"Every nation has offered to help uncover the murder nation. They flew radar-patrols and reported various suspicious sites, two of which we bombed without result. But the radar-patrol in a part of the South Atlantic was in the hands of the nation we had previously suspected. Its radar detected no bombs coming north from Antarctica. They did detect—and report—our bombs going south to Antarctica under identical conditions. But it is true that they reported our bombs as meteors. We believe that they deliberately concealed the indications of bombs moving against us. There was one other item, but—"

He turned to the men from Sun Valley, standing in the control room.

"Your verdict, please," he said.

The Englishman shifted the sheaf of papers which contained every detail of the evidence he had summarized—and the item he had not yet revealed. He swallowed.

"G-guilty. On my word, I believe it."

The Frenchman said, "On my honor, guilty!"

The Russian said it impassively. The Pole snarled it in triumphant hate. The Greek, the Chinese, the Hungarian. . . .

"We have already acted on our own conviction," said Sam with a bitter grimness. "In thirty seconds more our bombs will begin to fall. In five minutes or less yours will join ours, or we and all who do join us will believe you sympathize with our enemy! And —and—"

He looked at his wrist-watch. His hand shook again.

"Our bombs should be falling now. I give you the last bit of evidence. An electric motor in the enemy bomb was American made, by a great American company, which had many small factories scattered in small towns to make the small parts for its assembly-plants. The name-plate of the motor had been left on it, as a form of zestful joke. It contained, ac-

169

tually, a serial number. And by the quaintest of possible accidents, the small town that made that motor was not bombed. It was able to name the purchaser of two thousand similar motors made on special order—the War Department of the nation on which our bombs are dropping now!"

He stepped close to the microphone.

"Our enemy," he said steadily, "is—"

He spoke one word.

"*Whoooo-ooooo-OOOO-OOOOOOMMM!*" A bomb went screaming for the stars. "*Whooo-oooo-OOOO-OOOOOOMMM!*" went another. And now, with the precision-targets cared for by the carefully computed courses of the Math Room, a new type of course-setting took effect. Bombs went up now with a deliberately introduced factor of dispersion. They would fall within a certain area, but indifferently and at random within its limits. They would destroy open fields and tiny hamlets and forests and streams and everything that moved or lived or breathed. . . .

They went up faster since all the courses were set alike.

"*Whoooo-oooo-OOOOO-OOOOOOMMM!*"

"*Whoooo-oooo-OOOOOO-OOOOOOO-MMM!*"

"*Whoooo-oooo-OOOO-OOOOOOMMM!*"

Twenty-four hours later there was silence on a hilltop among the mountains. Men were at work not far away, dismantling a snapper-bomb emplacement, but they did not often appear above the curve of the hill. The sun shone very brightly, and a small bird quite absurdly hopped about on the barren stone. Sam Burton sprawled on the ground, with Betty Clarke sitting beside him. They did not speak. He was worn out, but relaxed in that almost painful relief that follows intolerable strain.

Far away, over the horizon, amateur radio operators were beginning to come back on the air. Local garages adapted motor generators for the recharging of batteries. The authorities of small municipalities were requisitioning motors which could be turned into dynamos for the purposes of communications. The Air Force was establishing a far-flung, hastily improvised network of air-lines, using bombers and scouts and its transport planes for the carriage of emergency cargo and passengers. Farmers cultivated their fields.

There were still monstrous craters sprawled across America. The scars would last forever. But there had been no invasion. There would not be. The United States was still free, and already minor politicians began to lay plans for intricate and devious political tricks by which they would come to the fore in the reestablished national government. And other men soberly considered the beginning of factories with the means at hand, and other men still. . . .

But up on the hilltop, Sam Burton slept the sleep of utter weariness. Betty watched over him gravely.

Presently she looked furtively around her, and bent over and kissed him.

www.ingramcontent.com/pod-product-compliance
Lightning Source LLC
Chambersburg PA
CBHW022121170626
46808CB00002B/796